HAR
Presents

Welcome to this month's books from Harlequin
Presents! The fabulously passionate series
THE ROYAL HOUSE OF NIROLI continues with
The Tycoon's Princess Bride by Natasha Oakley,
where Princess Isabella Fierezza risks forfeiting
her chance to be queen when she falls for
Niroli's enemy, Domenic Vincini. And don't miss
The Spanish Prince's Virgin Bride, the final part of
Sandra Marton's trilogy THE BILLIONAIRES' BRIDES, in
which Prince Lucas Reyes believes his contract fiancée
is pretending she's never been touched by another man!

Also this month, favorite author Helen Bianchin brings
you *The Greek Tycoon's Virgin Wife,* where gorgeous
Xandro Caramanis wants a wife—and an heir. In
Innocent on Her Wedding Night by Sara Craven,
Daniel meets his estranged wife again—and wants
to claim the wedding night that was never his. In
The Boss's Wife for a Week by Anne McAllister,
Spence Tyack's assistant Sadie proves not only to be
sensible in the boardroom, but also sensual in the
bedroom! In *The Mediterranean Billionaire's Secret
Baby* by Diana Hamilton, Italian billionaire Francesco
Mastroianni is shocked to see his ex-mistress again after
seven months—and she's visibly pregnant! In *Willingly
Bedded, Forcibly Wedded* by Melanie Milburne,
Jasper Caulfield has to marry Hayley or he'll lose his
inheritance. But she's determined to be a wife on paper
only. Finally brilliant new author India Grey brings you
her first book, *The Italian's Defiant Mistress*, where
only millionaire Raphael di Lazaro can help Eve—if she
becomes his mistress....

MISTRESS
TO A
MILLIONAIRE

*She's his in the bedroom,
but he can't buy her love...*

Showered with diamonds, draped in
exquisite lingerie, whisked around
the world in the lap of luxury...

The ultimate fantasy becomes a reality.

Live the dream with more
MISTRESS TO A MILLIONAIRE titles
by your favorite authors coming soon.

Available only from Harlequin Presents®.

India Grey

THE ITALIAN'S DEFIANT MISTRESS

MISTRESS
TO A
MILLIONAIRE

HARLEQUIN®

TORONTO • NEW YORK • LONDON
AMSTERDAM • PARIS • SYDNEY • HAMBURG
STOCKHOLM • ATHENS • TOKYO • MILAN • MADRID
PRAGUE • WARSAW • BUDAPEST • AUCKLAND

ISBN-13: 978-0-373-12674-3
ISBN-10:   0-373-12674-3

THE ITALIAN'S DEFIANT MISTRESS

First North American Publication 2007.

Copyright © 2007 by India Grey.

This edition published by arrangement with Harlequin Books S.A.

® and TM are trademarks of the publisher. Trademarks indicated with ® are registered in the United States Patent and Trademark Office, the Canadian Trade Marks Office and in other countries.

www.eHarlequin.com

Printed in U.S.A.

All about the author...
India Grey

A self-confessed romance junkie, **INDIA GREY**
was just thirteen years old when she first sent off
for the Harlequin writers' guidelines. She can still
recall the thrill of getting the large brown envelope
with its distinctive logo through the letterbox. She
subsequently whiled away many a dull school day
staring out the window and dreaming of the perfect
hero. She kept these guidelines with her for the
next ten years, tucking them carefully inside the
cover of each new diary in January, and beginning
every list of New Year's resolutions with the words
Start Novel.

In the meantime she gained a degree in English
literature and language from Manchester University,
and in a stroke of genius on the part of the gods of
romance, met her gorgeous future husband on the
very last night of their three years there.

The past fifteen years have been spent blissfully
buried in domesticity—and heaps of pink washing
generated by three small daughters—but she has
never really stopped daydreaming about romance.
She's just profoundly grateful to finally have an
excuse to do it legitimately!

For Penny, a real-life fairy godmother,
who showed me how to make
the dream come true.

CHAPTER ONE

'I CAN'T do this.'

Eve's voice was little more than a whisper as the icy hand of fear gripped her throat and trailed its chilly fingers down her spine. She wanted to run, but was suddenly too panic-stricken to move. Besides, in the stiletto-heeled thigh-length boots she probably wouldn't get very far.

On the other side of the curtains the ballroom of Florence's grandest *palazzo* was packed with five hundred of the world's most wealthy and beautiful, who had come to pay homage to the man who had been dressing them for half a century. Only the cream of Antonio di Lazaro's client list had been invited to attend this exclusive fiftieth anniversary retrospective, and any celebrities not sitting out there in the glittering ballroom waiting for the show to begin were backstage, getting ready to model some of the legendary Lazaro label's most iconic designs.

Sienna Swift, current supermodel darling of the international fashion scene, looked up briefly from the magazine she was reading and gave Eve her famously dazzling smile.

'Course you can. You'll be fine.'

'But I'm a…a journalist.' The dishonesty of the statement made Eve falter as she said it. 'My friend Lou was supposed to be doing this article—she'd have been fantastic, but I've never done anything like this in my life. I don't know the first thing about modelling!'

Sienna turned the page. 'Well, babe, you've got the legs for it. And better boobs than the rest of us put together. What's to know? It's hardly rocket science.' She paused to scrutinise a photograph of one of her closest rivals before adding, 'It's all about sex, I suppose.'

'Sex?' Eve wailed, her spirits sinking even further. 'Why sex? Where I come from sex is not something you do in front of five hundred people and photographers from every major publication around the globe.'

Apparently. She couldn't very well say she didn't know the first thing about that either.

Sienna sighed and put the magazine down.

'OK, we haven't got long, so let's make this as simple as possible. All you have to do is find someone to focus on. You're up there on the catwalk, right? And you just fix your eyes on some bloke and forget everyone else. Watch.'

The model took a couple of steps back, thrusting her hips forward in classic catwalk style and placing her hands on them. Looking around for a likely candidate, she fixed her smoky gaze on the singer from Italy's hottest new boy band, who'd just come offstage.

'You walk towards him and you never take your eyes off him,' she murmured through sultry, pouted lips. 'Not for a second. This is lust at first sight. You're looking at him as if he's the sexiest man alive and you're going to go right up to him and strip his clothes off and there and then.' She swung back to Eve with a wicked smile. 'That's all there is to it!' And to the obvious dismay of the blushing singer she picked up the magazine again and resumed her study of it.

Eve squirmed uncomfortably in the transparent PVC mini-dress, and tugged it down over her bottom. It would be a lot easier to follow Sienna's advice if she was allowed to wear her glasses, without which she wasn't going to be able to focus on anything more than half a metre away from her face, and if she wasn't dressed in an upmarket plastic bag. She seemed to have drawn the short straw in the clothes lottery, and had been allocated one of Lazaro's more bizarre creations from his *avant-garde* phase in the 1960s. Strategically positioned fluorescent flowers stopped the dress being absolutely X-rated, but she still felt horribly exposed.

All around her some of the most beautiful women in the world were sipping mineral water from miniature bottles and dropping the kind of names that would have sent a real journalist into a frenzy of excitement. Among them Eve felt lonely, disorientated, and about as glamorous as a transit van in a garage full of sportscars.

She didn't belong here.

She closed her eyes against the sudden wave of homesickness that threatened to knock her for six as she thought of her messy desk by the window in Professor Swanson's office. At this time of year her view of the college quadrangle was almost entirely obliterated by the wisteria rampaging across the window, casting a murky underwater light over the clutter of teacups and student essays and piles of scribbled notes in the dusty book-lined room.

That was her world, and she had been crazy to think for a second that she could cut it in Lou's. Fashion journalists—especially those who were successful enough to shadow supermodels for exclusive behind-the-scenes articles on the A-list events of the year—were generally not shy, shortsighted academics. There was just no way she could pull it off.

'I think I'd better go and get changed,' she muttered, trying to squeeze through the crush at the steps to the catwalk.

The plan had failed before it had even begun, and it was better that she face that fact now. Lou had taken a huge risk in faking illness at the last minute and putting Eve forward for this article, and if either of them had stopped to think about it they would have realised how outrageous the whole scheme was. She was going to let Lou down, but that wasn't the worst part.

The worst part was letting her twin sister Ellie down. And letting Raphael Di Lazaro slip through her fingers again.

Without looking up from the horoscope page, Sienna grabbed her arm and pulled her back. 'No time,' she said cheerfully. 'We're on in a second. Look, it says here that Scorpios should exercise caution in financial matters. Do you think that means I shouldn't buy that Prada clutch bag, then?'

Eve's teeth were chattering violently as she replied, 'I shouldn't think so. Look, it doesn't by any chance say that on Thursday Aquarians should avoid public displays of nudity and stay at home eating chocolate instead, does it?'

Sienna laughed. 'Let's see. Aquarius. "Due to Mercury moving into the pinnacle of your chart, Thursday will see a spectacular reawakening of your love-life. Your destiny awaits you in a most unexpected place." Excellent! You'd better stick around after all!'

Eve grimaced. Even if she could persuade herself to believe in astrology—or destiny, for that matter—she'd have to draw the line at reincarnation. Her love-life wasn't just sleeping, it was dead and buried.

No. If she was going to stick around it would be nothing to do with love or *destiny*, for pity's sake, and everything to do with revenge.

She gave Sienna a watery smile. 'Just my luck the man of my dreams is going to appear in my life the day I'm dressed as Porn Star Barbie.'

The grand ballroom of the Palazzo Salarino glittered in the light from its famous antique crystal chandeliers as the floor-length windows darkened from the blue of late afternoon to the deep mauve of evening. The body of the room was filled with row upon row of gilded chairs, seating the fashion world's premier figures, and the perfection of the scene was reflected in the numerous Venetian mirrors that lined the walls.

On shaking legs Eve stepped out from the wings.

For a second she couldn't see anything at all as a thousand flashbulbs dazzled her, and it was all she could do not to put her hands in front of her face to shield it. The catwalk stretched ahead of her, looking at least a mile long, and beyond it lay the elegant salon with its sea of upturned faces.

Sienna's words came back to her. *'Find someone to focus on...'*

Desperately she scanned the cavernous room, for once glad that her shortsightedness prevented her from recognising the dauntingly famous faces. Her steps slowed and she felt the smile freeze on her face. Was she supposed to smile? She couldn't remember. The audience was a whispering restless mass. It was impossible to single anyone out, Eve thought in panic, willing herself to keep going while every fibre of her being was telling her to turn on her spike heels and run.

Someone was standing in the shadows, leaning against one of the marble pillars with his head tilted back. He was wearing a dark suit that outlined the powerful breadth of his shoulders against the pale marble, and there was something incredibly arresting about his stillness. In the dimly lit room, through the fog of her shortsightedness, it was impossible to see him clearly, but she could feel his eyes upon her.

I can do this, she thought. *I can do this.*

Achingly beautiful, heartbreakingly poignant, the exquisite notes of *Madame Butterfly* drifted through the room, filling her with their bittersweet sexual yearning. She and Ellie had always loved this opera, sneaking to the top of the stairs in their nightgowns to catch this particular aria when their mother used to play it late at night on an old record player. The words were as familiar to her as a lullaby, and hearing them now gave her strength.

Everything around her receded—the cameras, the audience, the syrupy voice of the pink-suited host. The world shrank to encompass nothing but the music and the dark, narrowed eyes of the stranger. He didn't move, but as she swayed towards him she could feel the laser beam burn of his gaze and sense the sexual energy he gave off, like heat. It melted into her skin, making it tingle, thawing her icy shell of insecurity and shyness.

For the first time in two years she felt properly alive.

Reaching the end of the catwalk, she lifted her head and paused. Their eyes locked over the rows of people separating them in a dizzying moment of absolute sexual recognition. For a brief second Eve seriously considered keeping going: jumping down from the catwalk and walking right up to him, as Sienna had said. Her body was crying out to him with an urgency that took her breath away, and the need to touch him, to inhale his scent and taste the warmth of his lips, was almost overwhelming.

The photographers at her feet surged forward in a volley of flashbulbs. Blinded by white light, she could still see the dark silhouette of her mysterious rescuer imprinted on her mind. Wrenching her dazzled gaze away, she turned to walk back up the catwalk, still feeling his eyes upon her and helplessly aware of the wanton undulation of her hips. In the few seconds that their eyes had held he had insinuated himself under her skin, like some mystical enchanter, infusing every cell in her body with molten longing. She was possessed.

Stepping shakily off the catwalk, she slipped through the crowd of girls waiting to go on and, oblivious to their smiles and congratulations, stumbled back to her corner of the communal dressing area. Throwing herself into a chair, she stared at her reflection in the mirror.

She looked like Sleeping Beauty must have in the moment following Prince Charming's kiss—dazed, bewildered, and unmistakably aroused. Gone was the shy, uncertain girl who had stepped nervously through the curtains five minutes ago, and in her place was a tousled maenad with bee-stung lips and eyes like dark pools of invitation.

The horoscope had been spookily accurate. It was exactly as

if she had been sleeping until the electrifying presence of the unknown man had brought her painfully, pleasurably, back to consciousness.

She dropped her head into her hands. Except that clever, sensible Eve didn't believe in all that nonsense, did she?

She had been the shy twin, always in the shadow of flamboyant, confident Ellie. Ellie had been the one who'd devoured horoscopes and believed in destiny, pursuing your dream. While Eve had still been at Oxford, working hard on her dissertation, Ellie had abandoned her degree in Art History and blown her student grant on a one-way ticket to Florence instead.

She'd wanted to experience art and passion and beauty for herself, not hear about it second-hand in some dingy lecture theatre. At some point, when she'd been in Florence for a couple of months, she'd clearly decided to add heroin to the list of things she wanted to experience.

That was where following your dreams and reading your horoscope got you. To an anonymous, sordid death that the police hadn't even bothered to investigate.

They hadn't, so Eve had vowed she would. In the two years since it had happened Eve's life had shrunk even further, until there was nothing left but her work for Professor Swanson and the cold, aching desire for closure and for justice.

But the face that stared back at her from the mirror now was transformed by desire of a different kind. It was the face of a girl who knew what she wanted—and it had nothing to do with revenge. The expression in her eyes was one of white-hot, naked, take-me-and-damn-the-consequences lust.

And, what was more, it suited her. Now all she had to do was find her man and…

'You were brilliant! A total natural!'

Sienna kicked off killer six-inch stiletto heels and helped herself to a miniature bottle of champagne from one of the ice buckets that were dotted around the dressing room. On the other side of the curtain the audience were still clapping and cheering as she took a long, thirsty swig.

In a daze, Eve looked up. The show couldn't have finished already. That would mean she had just spent the last forty-five minutes lost in an erotic fantasy.

'Right, then,' Sienna went on happily, 'That's the work bit over. Now it's party time!' *Oh, God. She* had *just spent the last forty-five minutes lost in an erotic fantasy.* 'The Lazaro parties are always totally wild.' With an alarming lack of inhibition Sienna stripped off the outrageous white leather and tulle wedding dress she had worn for the finale and tossed it aside. 'Have you seen how many celebs are out there? I can't wait to meet them. And there's even a whisper going around that Rapahel di Lazaro is back from abroad. He's supposed to be, like, *so-ooo* gorgeous. I'm definitely going to introduce myself.'

The mention of *that* name brought Eve back to reality with roughly the same force as a head-on collision at high speed. He was the one she should be spending the evening trying to get close to, not her handsome hero.

'Well, if you find him you can introduce me too. I'd love to meet the mysterious Raphael di Lazaro. So far I haven't even been able to dig out so much as a photograph of him. How come he's so elusive?'

Sienna shrugged. She had changed into a backless, barely-there dress in cherry-pink, and was now slipping her feet into a pair of pink satin wedges that even Eve recognised as being the height of fashion.

'He left before I started modelling for Lazaro, but people here are still talking about him. The rumour goes that his girlfriend ran off with his brother—Luca; you're bound to meet him—and Raphael couldn't handle it. I heard he went to South America somewhere, though I'm not sure if that's right. I mean, he's a fashion photographer, and it's not an area you'd really associate with fashion, is it?'

Eve gave a dry laugh. 'No.' *Drugs, yes. Fashion, no.*

'Anyway, that's why he hasn't been around for a couple of years. And even before he went the paparazzi used to give him a pretty wide berth.' Sienna finished applying shocking pink lipstick and paused for a moment while she pressed her lips together. 'He *hates* them, apparently, but that's not unusual in this business. What's more surprising is that they seem to respect that. He must be quite a guy. Hey, Eve…? Are you all right?

'Oh. Yes. Yes, of course.'

'Well, come on, then. We're missing valuable party time! What are you wearing?'

'Oh, nothing much. I mean, not literally—but I've only got this.' Flustered, Eve got to her feet and rummaged inside a moth-eaten antique carpet-bag—her Mary Poppins bag as Ellie used to call it—fishing out a slither of silk which she tossed absent-mindedly to Sienna.

Sienna held the dress up carefully. 'It's gorgeous. Where's it from?'

Eve flashed her a smile and put on a posh, showbiz accent. 'A frightfully exclusive little label called Charity Shop. Frankly, darling, I never wear anything else.'

The lavender-scented air was still warm, and, stepping out onto the romantically lit terrace, Raphael Di Lazaro felt an enormous sense of relief. The ornate grandeur of the *palazzo*'s ballroom, with its wall-to-wall celebrities and trophy wives, had been suffocating. Everything was so highly polished and symmetrical, just like the perfectly made-up, expressionless faces of the models, but it made the dust and chaos he had so recently left behind in Columbia seem positively refreshing in comparison.

Accepting a glass of champagne from a passing waiter, he discreetly checked his watch. This was the kind of event he usually avoided like a hot day in hell, but he was here on business, not for pleasure. This was exactly the sort of environment in which his slimeball brother was most likely to operate.

Half-brother. Since uncovering evidence of the new depths of evil and corruption concealed behind Luca's shallow charm, Raphael was more determined than ever to remember that they shared only one parent. And Antonio Di Lazaro had played such a distant role in Raphael's upbringing that he hardly qualified for the title of father.

Luca was the golden boy in Antonio's eyes. In everyone's eyes.

Grimly, Raphael lifted his glass to his lips, as if the bubbles would wash away the bitter taste that always accompanied this train of thought. Draining it in one long draft, he was surprised to find that his habitual acrimony was tinged with sympathy. It wasn't going to be easy for Antonio to face the fact that his favourite son was facing charges of international drugs trafficking and money laundering. Especially when the money had most probably come from the Lazaro accounts.

But he was jumping ahead of himself. Luca hadn't been arrested yet, and Raphael was here to make sure that nothing happened to prevent that at this delicate stage of the operation.

Looking around for his father, he stifled a yawn. Even when he'd worked for Lazaro he'd despised this celebrity schmoozing, and his time in Columbia had only served to heighten his loathing of it. In fact today extreme tiredness and crashing boredom had made a pretty lethal combination, so that during the endless procession of identikit clotheshorses he'd almost fallen asleep.

Maybe he had, just for a moment. Maybe that astonishing erotic encounter had been nothing more than a dream...

He felt his tired body stir and stiffen at the memory of the girl in the transparent dress. Surely it was too vivid to have been a dream? He could still picture the terror in her huge eyes as she'd stepped into the lights of the catwalk, still remember the surge of protectiveness he'd felt towards her as she'd faltered, still feel the adrenalin rush that had crashed through him as she'd looked straight into his eyes…

Adrenalin? Who was he kidding? What he'd felt was a rush of pure testosterone. It wasn't just sleep deprivation he was suffering from.

OK, so there hadn't exactly been an endless supply of attractive, intelligent women to choose from in Columbia's underworld, and two years was a hell of a long time for any man without a burning religious conviction to behave like a monk, but he wasn't desperate enough to pick up some air-headed model. Bitter experience had taught him that models required the same kind of intensive, round the clock attention and affection as small children. And they were just as likely to get themselves into trouble if left unsupervised. It was a responsibility he wouldn't be stupid enough to take on a second time.

Suddenly his eyes narrowed as he caught sight of Antonio. Emerging onto the terrace, he was making his way slowly in Raphael's direction, surrounded by a small crowd of devotees. He was dressed as immaculately as ever, in a perfectly cut silvery-grey suit with his trademark white rose in the buttonhole, but Raphael was alarmed to see how much his father had aged in the time he had been away. As Antonio approached Raphael could see the unhealthy pallor of his lips, and the lines of exhaustion etched into his elegant, haughty face.

'Father.'

Caught off-guard, Antonio was unable to disguise his shock. Swiftly recovering his composure, he managed a chilly smile.

'Raphael. What a surprise. What are you doing here?'

'I had to come back for the Press Photography Awards in Venice on Saturday, but I have some business to attend to in Florence as well. Lazaro business, actually.'

Antonio's eyebrows rose a fraction. '*Si?* After all this time? You walked out on Lazaro two years ago, Raphael. I cannot imagine what business you would have here now.'

'I need to have a look at the company accounts.'

Antonio's eyes narrowed. 'You are short of money? Is that it? Maybe you should have thought of that before you left your job here to go off and photograph peasants in the back of beyond. Awards don't pay the bills, Raphael.'

A muscle flickered in Raphael's cheek. When he spoke, his voice was dangerously quiet. 'As far as I know I'm still listed as one of the company directors, so I am perfectly within my rights to have access to the accounts. Tomorrow, if that suits you. I'll need to see you once I've finished going through them.'

'Tomorrow is impossible. I have an interview about the retrospective with Italian *Vogue* in the morning, and the perfume launch in the afternoon.' Antonio looked suddenly exhausted, and seemed anxious to get away. 'Anyway, Raphael, you know how I loathe having anything to do with money. Luca is Financial Director, I leave everything to him. He's here somewhere—why don't you speak to him about it?'

'I'd rather not.'

'Don't be ridiculous. Luca is your brother. All that nonsense with Catalina is in the past—you can't still hate him for something that happened—what?—two years ago?'

Raphael felt his mouth twist into a sneer of contempt. 'Believe me, Father, I've discovered plenty more things to hate him for since then.'

But Antonio wasn't listening. With a dismissive wave of his hand in the direction of the *palazzo* he said, 'There he is. Sort something out with him.'

Luca Di Lazaro was leaning nonchalantly against the open French door, his broad frame filling the doorway and effectively blocking the escape of whichever unfortunate girl he had ensnared. Raphael's heart gave a lurch of pure loathing as he watched Luca lean down to say something to the girl. Something meaningless and flattering, no doubt. Something guaranteed to put her at her ease and charm her into a false sense of security.

It was a routine he had perfected on countless naïve young models over the years, as Raphael knew to his cost. His own girlfriend had been one of them, after all.

At that moment Luca shifted slightly to one side, coming to rest with deceptive ease, his back against the door frame. The movement gave Raphael a clear view of the girl he had trapped.

She had changed the transparent dress for a silk slip that, in hiding her delicious body, only seemed to emphasise its voluptuousness. The soft light from the room beyond cast a halo around the contours of her curves.

Adrenalin pulsed through him, hot and powerful. Without hesitating, or giving his father so much as a backward glance, Raphael found himself shouldering his way through the crowd towards them. Company accounts were the last thing on his mind as he wrestled with the primitive urge to push everyone out of the way, grab the girl from Luca and take her as far away as possible.

Luca straightened up as he approached.

'Well, well. The prodigal son returns.' His voice was slippery with sarcasm, and Raphael raked a hand through his hair in an attempt to stop himself punching that bland, handsome face. 'I would introduce you, but we've only just met and I haven't found out this beauty's name yet...'

Raphael's reaction was instant. Giving Luca a smile that would have frozen the Mediterranean, he turned to the woman with a light inclination of his head, praying she wouldn't give him away.

'*Cara?* Is there anyone else you'd like to meet, or are you ready to go?'

He allowed himself a small moment of triumph as he watched the look of surprise and something that resembled anxiety spread across Luca's face before turning his attention back to the girl.

Her eyes were the clear turquoise-green of old glass, and they glinted, catlike, in the light of the crystal chandeliers. Lust sliced through Raphael with the painless precision of a razorblade as he registered the spreading darkness at their centre.

There was the smallest hesitation before she replied. Her accent was English, her voice low and breathless.

'I'm all yours…darling.'

OK, for one night only Eve Middlemiss—BA hons and general clever clogs—was prepared to admit she'd been wrong.

There was such a thing as destiny. And he was standing right beside her.

They crossed the main reception area of the *palazzo*, his hand resting lightly in the small of her back, his thumb gently caressing the hollow at the base of her spine. Away from the main buzz of the party a few guests stood talking quietly in small groups, and uniformed staff hovered discreetly. Eve was dimly aware of their curious glances as she passed, but was almost beyond caring.

Almost. And then she remembered Ellie.

'I have to get back… I really shouldn't…'

As the words left her lips she knew they were completely unconvincing. She'd tried to adopt a firm, businesslike tone, but failed spectacularly. Something odd had happened to her voice, so that she sounded as if she was auditioning as a sex-line operator, and above the storm of hormone-fuelled emotions inside her a demonic alter-ego whispered, *Forget Ellie just for one night. Do something for your own sake for a change.*

He looked down at her. His face was completely expressionless.

'You don't, and you should. Believe me.'

His grip tightened on her waist, sending another shower of shooting stars down her spine and turning her stomach to water. She tried to laugh, but it came out as a gasp.

'I don't understand… I don't make a habit of this sort of thing…'

His beautiful mouth twitched into the ghost of a smile. 'Do you think that isn't obvious? That's exactly why I had to get you out of the clutches of that…low-life.'

'He seemed very charming.'

'Appearances can be deceptive.'

He pulled her into a quiet gallery off the main hallway, dimly lit by lamps placed on tables along the length of its walls. Just inside the door he stopped and turned to her, his face shadowed. God, her stomach wasn't the only thing he turned to water, she thought, feeling liquid heat seeping into the silk and lace of her tiny thong.

'Shouldn't I be allowed to decide that for myself?' she whispered.

His hair was raven-dark, falling over his forehead and accentuating the hollows beneath cheekbones that looked as if they had been chiselled in marble. Despite the perfection of his features, he carried with him an aura of exhaustion and despair, and she had to curl her hands into fists to stop herself reaching out and touching him, trying to soothe away the tension in his jaw and the haunted look in his dark eyes.

'I couldn't risk you making the wrong decision.'

'What makes you think I'd do that?'

He gave a hollow laugh. 'It's happened before.' Reaching out, he slipped a finger under the slender silk strap of her dress, which had slipped down her arm, and with infinite gentleness slid it back into place. In the silence Eve heard her own small whimper of longing as his fingers brushed her quivering skin.

Wrenching his hand away, he half turned, his haughty, aristocratic face a mask of reserve. Only the dark, glittering pools of his eyes betrayed his desire as he swung back to face her.

The moan that escaped him as his mouth found hers was the sound of a man surrendering control. His hands entwined themselves in the thick silk of her hair, pulling her to him, imprisoning her lips with his, so that her cries of naked desire were consumed in the furnace of his kiss. With savage urgency his tongue explored the velvet depths of her mouth, then, leaving her gasping her pleasure and desperation into the stillness of the empty room, moved downwards to her jaw, her neck, the perfumed, pulsing hollow at the base of her throat. Helplessly she felt her fingers sliding into his hair, willing him onward, downward, to where her nipples strained against the silk of her dress, yearning for the exquisite warmth of his mouth…

A discreet cough from the doorway stopped him in his tracks.

'Signor di Lazaro? Signor Raphael di Lazaro? *Scusi*, but it's your father. I'm afraid it's urgent.'

And then he was gone, leaving her dazed, disorientated, and struck dumb with horror.

This man wasn't her destiny. He was her nemesis.

CHAPTER TWO

It was just a small scrap of paper, torn from the back of a pocket diary or notebook.

Lying in the darkness beneath crisp hotel sheets, Eve held it close to her body, absentmindedly sliding it through her finger and thumb so that she could feel the difference in texture along the torn edge and the slight stiffness where at some point coffee been spilled on it.

She didn't need to switch the light on and look at it to know that the coffee stain was in the shape of a rather fat rabbit, or to read the numbers 592, which were the only remainders of the phone number that had once been written there. She had studied that scrap of paper in such minute detail so often over the last two years that she even knew that the smooth bit underneath her thumb right now was where the words *Raphael di Lazaro* were written. And just below and to the left of that, just by the rabbit's ear, was where it said *drugs*.

The girl Ellie had shared a flat with in Florence—Catalina someone or other—had sent her things back to England following her death, and when Eve had finally been able to face going through them she had found this tucked into one of the pockets of Ellie's jeans. The rest of the writing might have been consigned to eternal oblivion by the coffee, but Eve hardly needed to have it spelled out to her. These had to be the contact details of the person who had supplied Ellie with heroin. And that person was Raphael Di Lazaro.

By the time Eve had found the paper di Lazaro had already disappeared into darkest Columbia, and the Italian authorities had recorded a verdict of accidental death on Ellie and closed the case. But as far as Eve was concerned it wasn't over. She had vowed to expose Raphael di Lazaro for what he was, no matter how long it took her to do it. Which was why, when Lou had called her at work two days ago, to report that a paparazzi contact had spotted him arriving back at Florence's airport, she hadn't hesitated in going along with Lou's ridiculous plan. After all, strutting down a catwalk and pretending to be a fashion journalist were pretty insignificant hoops to jump through in order finally to come face to face with the man who was responsible for Ellie's death.

Her fingers tightened around the piece of paper until it was scrunched up in the palm of her hand. She had certainly succeeded in doing that.

Big style.

Face to face, lip to lip, body to body…

Oh, sweet heaven…

She started violently as her mobile phone burst into noisy life on the bedside table, letting out a shrill explosion of sound whilst simultaneously vibrating madly and glowing fluorescent green in the darkness. Eve made a clumsy grab for it, knocking over a glass of water in the process, and accidentally switching it on just as she swore graphically.

'Eve?'

Oh, God. It was Marissa Fox, editor of *Glitterati*, sounding terrifyingly brisk and efficient.

'Sorry. I mean—yes. Sorry'

Mercifully, Marissa cut her off mid-stutter. 'Look, Eve, I know the whole idea is that you're shadowing Sienna, but can I be an awful bore and ask you to tear yourself away from her for an hour or so and pop down to cover the press conference this morning?'

Eve sat bolt upright in the hope it would make her sound more awake. 'Press conference?' she echoed faintly.

'Yes, darling.' There was a steely edge to Marissa's voice that was more effective than any alarm clock. 'Di Lazaro's doctors are giving a press conference this morning on his prognosis. Not good, according to my sources.'

Squeezing her eyes tightly shut, Eve felt the blood drain from her head.

Was Raphael hurt?

'Eve? Are you still there?'

'Yes.'

'You *do* know that Antonio di Lazaro suffered a heart attack as he was leaving the party last night, don't you?'

'Antonio?' Relief flooded through her, followed by a wave of self-disgust. Why should she care whether Raphael was hurt or not? If someone else had got there first it would save her the bother of doing it herself. But deny her the satisfaction.

'Right. Yes, sorry—of course I knew that he'd been taken ill,' she lied hastily. 'Everyone I spoke to sort of played it down. Is it serious?'

'Well, you'll find that out at the press conference, darling,' Marissa replied acidly. 'Ten o'clock at the Santa Maria Nuova hospital. I'd go myself, but *miraculously* I've managed to get an appointment in the hotel spa for a Seaweed Body Wrap and Triple Oxygen Facial. I'll be cutting it fine for the perfume launch as it is.' She sighed heavily. 'Such a shame that Lou's got this hideous shellfish allergy—she's always rather good at the whole press conference circus. But I'm sure you can manage just as well—can't you, darling?'

Eve groped for her glasses and pushed them on, almost swearing out loud again as she squinted at her watch in the gloom. Nine-twenty.

'Press conference? Absolutely. No problem. I'll be there.' Stumbling out of bed, she made a huge effort to sound like the professional journalist that Lou had told Marissa she was. 'So…is it a…big press conference?' She pulled open the lavishly swagged curtains, wincing as bright sunlight highlighted the chaos in the room, and the fact that Sienna's bed was the only thing that was still neat and unused. 'Are we expecting… er…statements from just the medical team, or will the family be present as well?'

'Family? Good heavens, darling, I shouldn't think so. Antonio's heart attack didn't stop Luca partying till the early hours, so I doubt he'll be in any state to face the press—which just leaves Raphael, and he's utterly allergic to publicity in any form. He's quite pathologically anti-journalists and paparazzi. Ah! Here's breakfast. Do you know, darling, this is supposed to be Florence's *top hotel*, and they don't do wheatgrass juice! Can you believe it? Anyway, darling, must dash. Give my love to Sienna, won't you? Hope you're getting lots of juicy gossip for the interview—can't wait to see the copy. I'll catch up with you both at the launch. *Ciao*, darling!'

Head reeling, Eve exhaled slowly into the sudden silence, and for a moment considered throwing herself onto the bed and screaming very loudly into a pillow. It was tempting, but ultimately not very constructive. And right now she needed help.

Picking her way through the ankle-deep mulch of discarded designer clothing that was the only sign of Sienna's occupancy in the room, Eve speed-dialled Lou.

Waiting for her to pick up, Eve felt her panic start to subside. Lou would know what to do—about the press conference and the case of the disappearing supermodel and yesterday's embarrassing incident, where the guy she'd thought was the man of her dreams had actually turned out to be—oops, sorry—the dark figure who stalked her nightmares.

No. *No. Noooo! Please, please don't be…*

Voicemail.

With a wail of anguish Eve threw her phone down and stood motionless for a moment in the middle of the room, as the panic returned and threatened to overwhelm her. Lou always said that when things went wrong all you had to do was imagine a way in which they could be worse. At that particular moment Eve couldn't think of one.

But a minute later, examining her reflection in the enormous Hollywood-style bathroom mirror, she was spared the bother of trying.

Her face, above a skimpy T-shirt with a picture of Shakespeare on the front, was deathly pale, with last night's mascara still smudged beneath her eyes. Her hair, cut yesterday for the fashion show into what the stylist had called 'sexy tousled layers' was now so sexily tousled that she looked as if she'd enjoyed a non-stop, all-night love-fest. All things considered, out of the two of them it was Shakespeare who looked the livelier. And the more attractive. And he'd been dead for nearly four hundred years.

She had just fifteen minutes to turn the day around and transform herself into a sleek, professional fashion journalist.

Fifteen minutes…and the entire cosmetic collection of one of the world's hottest supermodels.

How hard could it be?

She might have left the hotel without her glasses, but it wasn't hard to find the conference room at the Santa Mariá Nuova hospital. All she had to do was follow the click-clack of kitten heels and the wafts of expensive fragrance of a hundred fashionistas.

Finding a space beside a tarty-looking blonde from one of the less salubrious celebrity gossip magazines, Eve rummaged in her bag for the little tape recorder Lou had lent her and, unable to see properly without her glasses, took three attempts to insert a new tape.

The blonde girl threw her a sympathetic glance. 'Tough night last night?'

'You could say that.'

'Me too. My hangover's so bad I could do with joining di Lazaro in Intensive Care.'

Eve smiled. Thankfully she was spared the necessity of explaining that she was suffering the after-effects of intoxication of a different kind by the appearance of a woman, and two men in doctor's coats on the platform at the front of the room. A searing flare of disappointment tore through her like a physical pain at the realisation that Raphael was not amongst them.

She *had* to see him again, she rationalised silently, gritting her teeth. What had happened last night had raised more questions than it had answered, and whichever way you looked at it she had a whole lot of unfinished business regarding Raphael di Lazaro.

Taking their places at a starched white table, the trio on the platform looked as if they were about to ask for the wine list. Eve recognised the woman from the retrospective as Alessandra Ferretti, Lazaro's formidable and deeply attractive press officer. She took the centre seat, with a doctor on either side of her, and for a moment the three of them spoke quietly between themselves, before Ferretti checked her watch and leaned forward to speak into the microphone in a ridiculously husky voice.

'*Buongiorno.*'

The army of reporters shifted expectantly, pens, cameras, tape recorders poised. But then a door at the back of the room opened, and everyone swung round to look at the latecomer.

Eve's gasp was lost in an explosion of flashbulbs and a deafening machine-gun rattle of shutters as every photographer in the room instantly went for a shot of Raphael di Lazaro.

His dark hair fell forward over his face. Shadows of fatigue and twenty-four hours of stubble emphasised the high, slanting cheekbones and the sulky, sensual mouth. Even unshaven, and in last night's rumpled dark suit and white shirt, he was still savagely, effortlessly attractive. His face, as he pulled out a chair and slumped into it, was perfectly expressionless, but, watching him rake back his hair with long, suntanned fingers, Eve thought that he looked infinitely weary.

Her insides turned liquid with a potent mixture of loathing and lust.

Alessandra Ferretti was introducing everyone, her sexy drawl making it sound as if she was matchmaking at a cocktail party.

'Dr Christiano is Signor di Lazaro's consultant, and Dr Cavalletti is head of the cardiac team who will be responsible for his care.' She gestured to the white-coated men, then turned to Raphael and laid a slim brown hand on his arm. 'Raphael di Lazaro returned from Columbia only yesterday, but he has been with his father throughout the night.'

A tiny shock pulsed through Eve that Alessandra should mention Columbia so casually, but it was quickly submerged by a wave of irritation at the proprietary way her hand still rested on Raphael's arm.

'What's Antonio's condition now?' asked a reporter from one of the Italian broadsheets.

'*Agiato,*' replied the doctor on the right—Eve was ashamed to realise that she hadn't been paying enough attention to remember which one it was. 'He is in the best possible hands.'

'What treatment will he be undergoing?'

The other doctor cleared his throat self-importantly and launched into an in-depth medical lecture that had all the English-speaking journalists utterly bewildered. At the end of the table Raphael was leaning back in his chair, distractedly drawing on a notepad, totally oblivious to the intense attention of the media and of every woman in the room.

He had the face of a tortured saint in some religious tableau, Eve decided miserably, unable to stop herself from staring at him, or responding to that same aura of desolation she had noticed last night. She had spent the last two years inventing slow and painful deaths for this man, and suddenly she found herself wanting to walk right up to him, hold his face in her hands and kiss away all the anger and pain that she saw there.

She shook her head irritably. *Maybe she'd been right yesterday. Maybe she really was possessed.*

'What about the perfume launch? Is it still going ahead?' a journalist from one of the British glossies was asking.

'We feel that Antonio would want it to,' Alessandra Ferretti said smoothly. 'He has lavished much attention on its planning, and some of the biggest celebrities across the globe are coming to celebrate the launch of *Golden*, Lazaro's most exciting perfume ever, in what promises to be a glittering event in every sense of the word.' Product plug over, she arranged her face into a compassionate smile and resumed a hushed, respectful tone. 'Antonio always puts Lazaro first. It is his life, and to do anything other than carry on with business as usual would be utterly disrespectful of all he has worked so hard to create.'

Her answer was followed by another cacophony of questions, most of them directed at Raphael. How long was it since he had seen his father? Had he come back from South America because he knew Antonio was ill? How had Antonio seemed earlier in the evening?

He answered briefly, his voice harsh with tiredness. Eve kept her head down and her tape recorder raised to catch his answers, fearing that all it would be picking up was the frantic beating of her heart. Beside her, the tarty blonde was desperately trying to get noticed to ask a question.

'Signor di Lazaro! Raphael!'

Suddenly he looked in her direction. Eve froze.

'Where were you last night when Antonio was taken ill?'

'At the retrospective.'

Eve didn't dare breathe. If she kept her head down and stayed completely still perhaps he wouldn't notice her. If only the damned girl beside her would shut up and let him move on to someone else. But she was still talking. A vaguely insinuating note had crept into her voice.

'According to staff at the Palazzo Salarino, it took some considerable time to locate you. What were you doing?'

The silence that followed seemed to go on for ever. Slowly, and with a paralysing sense of dread, Eve dragged her eyes upwards from their intense study of the pattern on the carpet. And found herself looking straight into his.

It was like running at full speed into a wall of ice.

His expression was utterly blank as he held her in his dark gaze. Excruciating, yet indescribably erotic, like being intimately caressed while lying on a bed of nails. His voice, when he eventually replied, was very soft.

'That, it suddenly appears, is a very good question.'

For a second Raphael thought that tiredness had got the better of him and he was hallucinating. But there was no mistaking those eyes, or the softly rounded lips that had filled his head with pleasure during the long hours he'd spent, halfway between sleeping and waking, in a chair at his father's hospital bedside.

So she wasn't a model. It was even worse than that.

She was a journalist.

His grip tightened on the pen in his hand as a wave of self-recrimination swept through him. Going too long without sleep had made him irrational and careless, but that was no excuse for his stupid behaviour last night. Thank goodness that the *maître d'* had found him before things had gone any further, otherwise he might have been waking up to his name all over the front pages in headlines featuring the words 'passion', 'playboy', and probably 'love-rat'.

He looked across to where she stood, head bent, her face partly hidden by a curtain of hair, the tip of her pen held between her softly parted lips, and felt his heart—along with other more basic parts of his anatomy—harden.

In his eyes journalists came a little below single-cell organisms in the evolutionary scale. Just because this girl had the wide-eyed innocence of a blonde Virgin Mary, it would be unwise to rule out the possibility that she might still attempt to concoct some kind of kiss-and-tell story. He would just have to track her down and make sure she didn't.

She'd have her price. They all did. That was what was so disappointing.

'Taxi! Taxi!'

Eve let out a shriek of outrage as yet another of Florence's distinctive white cabs sped past her. That made five. She was beginning to wonder if she might just be invisible.

But of course she wasn't. If she were she would have been spared public humiliation at the hands—or eyes—of Raphael Di Lazaro.

How dared he? she spluttered inwardly. How *dared* he *look* at her like that? As if she was some kind of inferior life-form from the Planet Vulgar, and way beneath his contempt?

'Taxiii!'

If the street had not been crowded with intimidatingly glamorous Italian women, looking cool and inscrutable behind their designer sunglasses, Eve would almost certainly have sat down on the pavement and given in to tears. As it was, there was only one thing left to do.

Find chocolate.

The café nearby was small—just a handful of tables spilling out onto the pavement—but the enticing aroma of fresh coffee and hot pastries was irresistible. Taking her place in the queue of beautiful people at the counter, Eve wondered why everyone in Florence was so annoyingly good-looking. She had just arrived at the conclusion that Calvin Klein must be doing a casting session nearby, when, from the depths of her bag, she heard the tinny trill of her mobile.

Clamping her purse beneath one arm, she dug beneath the layers of old bus tickets, leaky Biros and odd gloves, triumphantly managing to unearth it before it stopped ringing.

'Lou…!'

'Hi, babe. You tried to call me. Everything OK?'

'Where were you? I needed you!'

'I was here. I'm just not answering my phone in case it's Marissa. I'm supposed to be at death's door, remember? The trouble is I got quite carried away with the story when I rang her to tell her, and now I can't remember all the details. Anyway, never mind that. How's it going?'

At the comfortingly familiar sound of Lou's voice Eve felt the sting of tears at the back of her eyes again. The need to offload was overwhelming.

'It's awful. I've completely messed everything up!'

'God, Eve, you'd better not have. Marissa will strangle me with one of her garish designer scarves if she finds out I made up all that stuff about your past modelling success and your dazzling journalistic career. Tell me it's not that bad.'

Eve swallowed nervously.

'Remember the time you interviewed that Hollywood movie star and spent the whole time giving him your come-get-me smile—then found out afterwards that you had lettuce stuck to your teeth? Well, it's about a thousand times worse than that.'

There was a painful pause. 'I don't believe you. But I'm listening.'

Miserably waiting in the queue, Eve watched the sultry girl behind the counter sprinkle chocolate on the top of a cappuccino. Even the waitresses round here looked like supermodels. She held the phone closer to her mouth and dropped her voice to a whisper.

'I kissed Raphael di Lazaro.'

'Sorry? I can't hear you. For a moment I thought you said you *kissed* Raphael di Lazaro!' Lou laughed heartily, and then stopped abruptly. 'Eve? Oh, God—that *is* what you said, isn't it?'

'Yes.'

'OK. Well, in that case I suppose just one question springs to mind—'

'Fantastic,' Eve whispered, staring straight ahead as the tears gathered in her eyes again. 'He's totally not how you'd expect.'

'*No*, Eve! The question was not, What was it like? The question was, In the name of Aunt Fanny, *why*?'

'Oh. I didn't know who he was at the time.'

'Now, wait a minute. I've known you since we both started university, and in all that time, Eve Middlemiss—four years of prime mating opportunities—I have never once known you to snog a guy without first meeting his mother and practising your new signature for after you're married.'

'That's not fair! I—' Eve hissed vehemently into the phone, but was unable to protest further as she'd reached the front of the queue at the counter. Hastily she ordered a chocolate croissant and a double mochaccino latte, adding sulkily, 'With extra cream.'

'Let's be honest, Eve.' Lou spoke more kindly now. 'You're not the kind of girl who kisses strangers. What's going on?'

'I don't know, Lou. It was bizarre—like fate, or destiny, or something. I saw him... No, we saw *each other*, and it was like something just clicked. It felt right. Inevitable, somehow. Like I didn't have to *do* anything because we both knew it was going to happen. It *had* to happen. And it did. After the show I was talking to this guy and, well, I know it sounds stupid, but *he* arrived and just sort of swept me away...'

'And you went with him? Just like that? Jeez, Eve!'

'I know, I know. It was stupid,' snapped Eve, wedging the phone against her ear as she handed money to the supermodel waitress. 'But at the time I was—I don't know—powerless to resist. You don't know what he's like, Lou... There's a sort of strength about him...'

'There was a "sort of strength" about Adolf Hitler too, but it hardly made him the ideal partner. Look, Eve, I don't like the sound of this. What happened last night was nothing to do with destiny, or love at first sight, or whatever fluffy notions you've got. It's far more likely that he remembers Ellie and recognised you, and intends to keep you quiet. It's not safe. I think you should come home.'

'No.' It came out more forcefully than she had intended, and the waitress gave Eve an odd look as she handed her the paper bag containing the croissant. Tucking it under her chin while she waited for her change, Eve continued in an urgent whisper, 'I'm not giving up now. For two miserable years I've waited to find out something, *anything*, that would bring me closer to understanding what happened to Ellie, and now I'm here and I've finally managed to put a face to the name on that bloody scrap of paper. And suddenly none of it seems to fit, and I don't know what I believe any more, but one thing is certain…' Her voice was rising as her resolve increased and, snatching up her hot chocolate, she swept away from the counter. 'I'm not coming home until I find some answers, whatever that takes. Either I'm going to expose di Lazaro as a sleazy drug pusher, or—'

She paused for a second to take a tentative sip of the froth on the top of her chocolate, closing her eyes in pleasure at the rich, sweet aroma. The next moment she had collided with something hard and unyielding.

A tidal wave of hot chocolate spilled over her hand, and made five small splashes on the front of the white shirt three inches from her nose.

The creased, obviously expensive, instantly recognisable white shirt three inches from her nose.

She gave a tiny whimper of distress.

'What? Eve? *Eve?*'

In one swift movement Raphael Di Lazaro had relieved her of the dripping paper cup and extracted her mobile phone from between her ear and her shoulder. His face was dangerously calm as he spoke into it, but his eyes glittered with anger.

'I'm afraid your friend seems to be momentarily lost for words, but let me reassure you that she's perfectly all right.'

Eve's cheek burned where his fingertips had brushed it, and she felt dizzy as she caught a brief hint of the scent of his skin. Vaguely, from the depths of her despair, she could make out the alarm in Lou's voice at the other end of the phone.

'Thank goodness for that. What happened?'

'It's nothing. Just a little accident with some hot chocolate. Tell me, is she always this clumsy?'

Eve heard Lou laugh, relaxing in the warmth of that low, impossibly sexy voice. Traitor. She wouldn't be so amused if she knew who she was talking to.

'Is she wearing her glasses?'

Raphael's chilly gaze flickered over Eve's face. 'No.'

'Oh, she's hopeless. Really, she shouldn't be allowed out on her own.'

'I couldn't agree more, *signorina*.'

Furious, Eve snatched the phone back. 'OK, Lou—lovely to talk to you. But you'd better go and sleep it off now. And remember—no more vodka at breakfast time.'

Snapping the phone shut with grim satisfaction before Lou could protest, Eve steeled herself to look up at Raphael. Even though he still wore that careful, guarded, blank expression, there was no mistaking the hostility it masked.

'So, Signorina Middlemiss…' He paused, enunciating each word very carefully, as if trying not to lose control of his temper. 'Perhaps you'd like to tell me exactly what you think you're doing?'

Her chin shot up in defiance. 'It was an accident—hardly anything to make a fuss about. I'm sure it'll wash out—'

His voice cut through her like the lash of a whip. 'Don't be childish. You know perfectly well what I'm talking about. What were the words you used? Sleazy drug pusher? I hardly think that's the sort of thing the readers of *Glitterati* want to hear about.'

The searing contempt in his tone was like acid on an open

wound. But even more painful was the realisation that Lou's theory might be right.

'So you do know who I am? Surprise, surprise. I might have known that men like you have spies everywhere.'

He raised a hand. For a crazy, delicious, dizzying split second she thought he was going to pull her into his arms and kiss her, as he had done last night. She was horrified at the disappointment that sliced into her as his fingers merely brushed the press ID badge clipped to the front of her scoop-necked T-shirt.

'"Eve Middlemiss. Fashion Assistant. Glitterati",' he read softly, his beautiful mouth curving into a cruel half-smile. 'One hardly has to have a sophisticated intelligence network to find these things out. Five minutes ago I knew almost nothing about you, *signorina*, but a picture is rapidly emerging.'

'Oh, yes? What picture?'

Damn. Only a complete simpleton would walk into that one. She could smell the sandalwood maleness of him, and it was having a catastrophic effect on her ability to think rationally.

'That of a silly, inexperienced journalist on a low-rent publication who is getting involved in things that are completely over her pretty blonde head.'

Well, she had asked.

He took a step back, making Eve suddenly aware of how close together they had been standing, and how the sheer nearness of him had held her spellbound. With space to breathe, the impact of his words suddenly hit her with all the force of a prizefighter's punch.

'You patronising male chauvinist *pig*! How dare you pass judgement on me?'

He had taken something out of his pocket and was leaning on one of the pavement tables, writing.

'Do you really want me to answer that?' he drawled, without looking up. 'Even your friend is of the opinion that you shouldn't be out on your own.'

'My *friend* was *joking*,' Eve hissed though gritted teeth. 'To understand that you need something called a sense of humour.'

Straightening up, Raphael leaned his elegant slim-hipped frame against the table and looked at her for a moment through narrowed eyes. Then, folding his arms in an attitude of complete ease, he began to talk in a swift stream of Italian. His voice was husky and low, almost caressing in its intimacy, and the words flowed over her like warm rain, making her skin tingle and the hairs stand up on the nape of her neck. For a blissful moment she felt an echo of the drenching pleasure that she'd experienced last night in his arms.

And then she realised he'd stopped speaking and was looking at her questioningly. 'So?'

Bewildered, mesmerised, she faltered and shook her head confusedly. 'I… Sorry, I…'

He had the same unruffled stillness about him as a panther reclining in the savannah: a dangerous watchfulness that, even though he was relaxed, made him look as if he could pounce at any moment.

'So. You don't speak the language. You don't know what you're getting into. You're out of your depth. Go home.'

'Are you threatening me?'

He sighed, and suddenly looked very tired. Noticing it, Eve felt again that irrational, treacherous pull inside, and her fingertips burned with the need to touch him.

'No, I'm warning you to be sensible.' He shook his head wearily. 'Please take this. I don't know how much you were hoping to earn from your little "scoop", but I think twenty thousand should more than cover it—don't you?'

'What?' she gasped, her momentary weakness evaporating in a fresh blast of fury. 'You're offering me twenty thousand euros to shut up and go home like a good girl?'

He gave her a sardonic smile. 'You underestimate my generosity. I'm offering you twenty thousand pounds.'

Speechless with shock, she glared at him for a long moment as tears pricked behind her eyes and her breath caught in her throat, choking the words that swirled around her head. *My sister's life was worth more than that!*

A taxi was speeding towards them, and she ran forward to hail it. But her tears and the forgotten glasses, combined with her desperate need to get away from him, made her clumsy. There was a screech of brakes and a blaring of horns as the taxi swerved to avoid her. In a split second Raphael was beside her, grasping her arms and pulling her back onto the pavement.

'*Voi ragazza piccola stupid,*' he spat. 'You stupid little child! You could have been killed!' He was still gripping her arm, and the icy cool of a few moments ago had been replaced with blistering fury. 'Do you not even know that in Florence you don't flag down taxis as you do in London? *Dio*, Eve!'

Ashen-faced, and with tears of humiliation and defeat coursing down her face, she looked up at him. 'Let me go. Please.'

She was still trembling. From shock, and maybe a little from the way he'd said her name, which on his lips sounded like Eva. But also from the realisation that he'd just jumped out into the road to save her life.

He did as she asked, stepping abruptly back as if she were the carrier of a contagious disease. With deliberate calm she turned back towards the road and held out her arm as a taxi came towards her. *Please, God, let this one stop. Please show Raphael di Lazaro, who clearly thinks he's your second-in-command, that he doesn't have to get everything right all of the time...*

She could have kissed the driver as he pulled up alongside her. She turned to Raphael, bravely trying to muster a smile through her tears.

'You see! I'm perfectly capable of—'

She gasped as he reached towards her and brushed his thumb across her lips in a gesture of perfect sensual intimacy. Her eyelids fluttered closed in blissful submission as, for a fraction of a second, she let her lips press against his firm flesh, feeling his warmth, tasting the salt-sweetness of him, unable to stop the cascade of heat that tumbled through her.

Her eyes flew to his, but found them cold and mocking.

'Froth. You were saying?'

His mouth curled into that cruel half-smile as he opened the door for her, then leaned over to speak to the driver. He took a fat wad of notes from his pocket and handed them over.

Furiously, she slammed the door and wiped her hand over her mouth, as much to dispel the feel of his thumb upon her lips as to remove any lingering traces of froth.

'What did he say to you?' she asked the driver as he pulled out into the stream of traffic.

'He ask me how much to airport. Is that where we go?'

'No! Take me to my hotel, please.'

'You sure, *signorina*? The *signore*, he pay me much money to go to airport.'

'I'm sure.'

It was a lie. Right now she would have done anything to skip the perfume launch, get on a plane home and never hear the word Lazaro again.

CHAPTER THREE

EVE wouldn't have thought it possible to be sitting in a gold limousine *en route* to a fearsomely exclusive A-list fashion event and have that horrible sick-in-the-stomach feeling she got on the way to the dentist.

On the seat opposite, Sienna stretched out her phenomenally long legs and sighed theatrically into her mobile. She'd spent the entire journey on her phone to either her agent or her film star boyfriend, and although Eve knew she should have been listening carefully for material to use in the article, her mind kept drifting back to her own problems.

Which was hardly surprising. Given the scale of them.

On paper all the evidence was falling neatly into place, and the fact that three hours ago Raphael di Lazaro had offered her more money to do nothing than Professor Swanson paid her for a year of hard work and long hours was another reason to believe in his guilt. And yet...

And yet the man she had glimpsed beneath that chilly, reserved veneer was neither evil nor corrupt. He had integrity. And he had it in spades.

Eve rested her forehead against the limousine window and shut her eyes, delicately probing the painful possibility that she was mistaking Raphael di Lazaro's undoubted good-looks and dazzling sex appeal for something more meaningful. A year or so ago, before she'd landed the job on the *Glitterati* fashion desk, Lou had done an article on women who fell in love with prisoners on Death Row. Over a bottle or two of cheap red in a wine bar in Oxford, Eve and Lou had discussed this phenomenon, snorting in contemptuous pity at the idea that anyone could let their heart rule their head in such a spectacularly foolish way.

Was she similarly deluded?

But she hadn't imagined the sheer strength that had held her and guided her as she'd walked down the catwalk just as surely as if his arms had been around her. Or the haunted need that lay just behind the expressionless public mask. Or the bone-deep, instinctive courage that would make him step out and grab her from the path of an oncoming car...

No! She banged her head softly but emphatically against the glass, as if to knock the sense back into it once and for all. The facts spoke for themselves. His name was on that paper, right above where it said *drugs*. He had followed her after the press conference and tried to buy her off.

Rational, intellectual Eve pressed her fingers to her temples and took a steadying breath. No matter what her heart was saying, her head knew perfectly well that he was still the most likely suspect. She had come to find answers, and she was still determined to do that. She just hadn't anticipated how painful it was going to be.

Sighing, she dragged her attention back to Sienna, who was thoughtfully examining a glossy acrylic nail. 'Will it involve taking my clothes off?' she was saying, still on her mobile—though whether it was to the agent or the boyfriend, Eve couldn't be sure. The glamorous model looked sensational, in spray-on white trousers and a diaphanous gold chiffon top that fell in soft, semi-transparent folds from a gold beaded choker at the neck. Only Eve would know that it had taken half an hour to construct her perfect cleavage with tape, and that much of the luxuriant black hair was, in fact, nylon extensions.

Nothing is as it seems on the surface, Eve thought bitterly.

They were close enough now to be able to see celebrities emerging from cars like gilded butterflies from their chrysalises. Everyone was faithfully sticking to the theme, and from the women's barely-there dresses to the men's over-the-top tailoring and salon tans the red carpet was transformed into a sea of gold.

Eve's own wardrobe was a little light on glitz, so Sienna had offered to lend her something from her own seemingly endless supply of clothes. It had been a kind offer but, coming as it had from a six-foot supermodel with a chest as flat as an ironing board, not remotely helpful. In the end Eve had been forced to resort to her faithful old jeans and jewelled Indian flip-flops, teamed with the only vaguely metallic-coloured thing she owned—a little vintage lace-trimmed camisole top from the 1930s, its cream silk darkened with age to a deep biscuity gold. In spite of the heat she'd fully intended to throw a jacket over the top, but Sienna had absolutely forbidden it, frogmarching her from the room without listening to her cries of protest.

'Of course you don't look like a hooker! This, in case you hadn't noticed, is *the look* of this summer. Honestly, Eve, I thought you were supposed to be a fashion journalist!'

Good point. She'd allowed herself to get so preoccupied with Raphael Di Lazaro she'd almost forgotten.

The car glided to a halt and Sienna gracefully unfolded her long limbs and stepped out. Waiting nervously for the paparazzi storm that heralded Sienna's arrival to subside before she stepped out of the safety of the limousine herself, Eve tried to arrange her face into a confident smile, but found her efforts considerably hampered by the sticky gold lipgloss Sienna had persuaded her to wear.

Drifts of sand specially imported from Egypt edged the red carpet and rose in mini-dunes at the entrance to the store, which was flanked with two enormous statues of the sphinx. But even this display of extravagant kitsch didn't prepare Eve for the spectacle that awaited them inside.

'What do you think?' yelled Sienna above the din, gesturing around them. 'Didn't I tell you the Lazaro parties are always wild?'

'It's unreal!' said Eve, looking round. Against a backdrop of gilded palm trees and faux-pyramids, A-list celebrities were being sprayed with *Golden* by scantily clad 'Egyptian' slave-girls, in Cleopatra-style wigs and scarlet lipstick. The air was heavy with the perfume, which smelt like a mixture of fruit salad and ozone.

In the centre of the floor a vast three-tiered fountain, topped by Tutankhamen's head, gushed champagne. A youth in a loin-cloth appeared beside them, proffering a plate of canapés. Forbidden by Sienna from wearing her glasses, Eve peered short-sightedly at them.

'What on earth are they?'

'South Sea tiger prawns in a vodka marinade, finished with eighteen-carat-gold leaf,' said the youth.

'Gold leaf?' echoed Eve faintly.

Sienna giggled. 'No, thanks. I'm catching a plane this evening. Don't want to set off the metal detectors. Come and get a drink,' she shouted to Eve, disappearing into the seething mass of exotically dressed celebrities.

It was impossible to squeeze through the crowd around the champagne fountain. Eve found herself alone on the fringes, craning above a hundred glossy, seriously high-maintenance heads to see where Sienna had gone.

Suddenly an arm snaked round her waist from behind. She whirled round to look into the laughing bloodshot eyes of the man from the retrospective. The man Raphael had been so keen to steal her away from.

'We meet again, *angel*. I see you standing here all alone, and I wonder how my brother could be so careless as to leave you unattended in the midst of such…' he looked around with a wolfish grin '…debauchery. You are like a beautiful rose blooming in a vase of artificial flowers.' His eyes moved lazily up and down her body for a moment, while a slow smile spread across his face.

'You're Raphael's brother?'

'*Si*. Half-brother. Though twice as charming. Luca di Lazaro.'

She took the hand he extended towards her. 'Eve Middlemiss.'

'Beautiful,' he murmured, looking very pleased about something and holding onto her hand for far longer than was necessary. 'And where is Raphael?'

'I'm not sure.' Eve managed a sort of grim smile, in spite of the lipgloss. 'But I'd like to find him.'

'Don't rush off, *bella*. Let me get you a drink. Is very hot in here, no? We need a passionfruit daiquiri!'

'I don't really…'

'Don't worry, *bambino*,' he soothed, laying a hot hand on her bare shoulder. 'It has hardly any alcohol. You'll love it. Trust me.'

In his father's private office on the top floor, Raphael held out the remote control, flicking from one CCTV image to another. Antonio had invested in the very best technology available to ensure that the Lazaro security system was state-of-the-art. Cameras were placed in strategic positions on each of the store's three floors, and also covered a large area of the street outside, and the information they generated was closely monitored by a highly trained team.

Raphael had considered briefing them on the necessity of keeping close tabs on Luca, but decided against it. The fewer people who knew about the investigation into his brother's drug dealing the better. This was one job he could not entrust to anyone else, and if Luca made one suspicious move, or got too close to anyone, Raphael would be watching.

His eyes were gritty and his whole body ached with fatigue. The ordeal of the press conference he had planned to return to his apartment for a few hours of much-needed sleep, but the encounter with Eve Middlemiss had put paid to that.

How much did she know?

His first thought when he'd seen her at the press conference was that she was a scheming, unscrupulous journalist who'd got the little-girl-lost act down to award-winning standard. Now he wasn't so sure. Her naïvety…her total bloody cluelessness…was way too realistic to be put on. And yet somehow she knew enough to blow an international drugs investigation sky-high.

He sighed and passed his hands briefly over his face. The situation with Luca was volatile enough without having an airhead blonde journalist set on writing some half-witted exposé charging around like a bull in a china shop.

No, that was all wrong. Not a bull… Something far more dangerously delicate than that. A fawn, perhaps. She was like a fawn careering through a minefield. The memory of her wide, frightened eyes as she'd stepped in front of the taxi came back to him, followed swiftly by the feel of the soft swell of her breast beneath her T-shirt as he'd pulled her back.

He shifted uncomfortably in his chair as a flicker of desire licked though him, and turned his attention abruptly back to the CCTV monitor. It didn't really matter what metaphor you chose. The fact remained that Eve Middlemiss was a problem. A complication he could well do without.

His mouth set in a grim line of contempt as he studied the screen. The scene it showed was like a nightmarish cross between a third-rate porn movie and a big-budget blockbuster. A very high-profile footballer's wife and an Oscar-tipped Hollywood starlet were cavorting in the champagne fountain as a crowd of onlookers clapped and cheered. Raphael's gaze skimmed dismissively over them, coming to rest instead on the knot of people around the fountain.

Only the tension in his broad shoulders betrayed the s of his ruthlessly controlled emotion as he located

Raphael didn't flinch, but the light from the screen showed the sudden shuttered stillness of his face as he watched his brother pick a strand of hair from the slickly glossed lips of Eve Middlemiss. She was looking up at Luca trustingly, her lips pouting and slightly parted, and once he had moved the stray hair, with much careful concern, she tentatively pressed them together. It was a movement that was curiously childlike, but at the same time piercingly erotic.

Gripping the remote control, Raphael saw his knuckles show bone-white through the suntanned skin of his hands. Dimly, as if from a great distance, he was aware of the pounding blood in his ears. He was a man who lived on his instincts, whose survival in the volatile Columbian underworld of drugs gangs and hired killers had depended on his ability to make split-second decisions. Every nerve and fibre of his being was telling him to go down and drag Eve Middlemiss away from Luca.

Now.

But of course it was out of the question. He pulled a hand across his stinging eyes, concentrating on thinking rationally. He'd tried to warn her. She wouldn't listen. She was, contrary to appearances, a grown-up, for goodness' sake. If she chose to play Russian Roulette with the devil all he could do was try to anticipate when the gun was going to go off.

He checked his watch. The party would last maybe two hours—that was about the maximum length of a celebrity's attention span. Leaning back in his chair, he resigned himself to his vigil.

All sense of time was suspended as he switched into professional mode and operated on automatic pilot. With ice-cold detachment he followed Eve and Luca's progress though the party, watching every gesture, tracking every drink, noting every movement. Throughout he remained motionless, unblinking and completely impassive.

Until the moment Luca put his jacket around Eve's bare shoulders and drew her, swaying slightly, towards the exit.

And then, letting out a stream of Italian expletives, Raphael was across the room and out of the door in seconds.

CHAPTER FOUR

IT WAS rush hour.

Sitting in the stream of slow-moving traffic, Raphael swore quietly under his breath. His hunch was that Luca would be taking Eve to the exclusive nightclub where the Lazaro party would continue into the small hours—one of Luca's favourite haunts. Raphael wondered how many girls had taken the first steps on the road to addiction hell in its opulent darkness.

He glanced at his watch. The traffic ahead was barely moving, and it had been just over ten minutes since he'd watched them leave.

Taking an abrupt right turn into a narrow sidestreet marked Senso Vietato—No Entry—he accelerated through the dustbins and empty cardboard boxes.

The backstreets ran parallel to the wide open space of a *piazza*, and Raphael weighed up the possibility of cutting right across it. On one hand it would get him to where he needed to be in half the time, on the other he was much more likely to attract the attention of the *polizia* and be pulled over. And what would happen to Eve then?

She would just be one more in the countless number of girls whose lives Luca had wrecked. Only this time Raphael would alert his contacts in the drug squad and make sure that they were onto him. Once they had caught Luca in the act, as it were, they would have the evidence they needed to make an arrest, and, since Luca was certainly not the kind of honourable person who would keep the names of his associates to himself, he would bring the whole morally bankrupt lot of them down with him.

It was an appealing thought.

One more girl. Surely it was a price worth paying? He should just pick up his mobile and dial the contact number he'd been given. They could have a team of undercover officers at the nightclub in no time.

In his head it was all so obvious.

But somewhere deep inside him something was telling him that Eve Middlemiss wasn't just one more girl. Raphael Di Lazaro was far too accustomed to burying his emotions to consider the possibility that it might be his heart.

As she walked arm-in-arm with Luca along the edge of the *piazza*, Eve peered into the little gold rope-handled carrier she had been given as they left the party and gave a little skip of delight. It wasn't just the absence of her glasses that was making the whole business of focusing the teeniest bit difficult, but she could have sworn that the writing on the little box which nestled beside the miniature bottle of *Golden* said 'Tiffany'.

'Ooh, Luca—look!' She beamed, extracting it from layers of tissue. 'Grown-up jewellery!'

The next moment there was a screech of tyres as a dark blue sports car appeared from one of the narrow side-streets and skidded to a halt inches away from them. Slamming a fist down on the bonnet, Luca hurled a stream of abuse at the driver.

'*Idiota!* Are you blind? Can you not read? It's a pedestrian zone, you—'

He stopped and gave a snarl of fury as the car door opened and Raphael got out. His face was deathly pale but his eyes blazed.

'Don't you ever give up, Luca?'

The malice in Luca's voice made Eve shudder. 'Lighten up,

for once in your miserable life, Raphael. When are you going to see that you can't just treat women like inconvenient items of luggage, and abandon them whenever it suits you? This little beauty was all alone so I looked after her, kept her amused. You should be grateful!'

'Looked after her? *Benedetta Maria.*' Raphael shook his head helplessly and turned to Eve, addressing her with icy calm. 'Can you not find a way to amuse yourself that doesn't involve a near death experience?'

'Excuse *me*?'

'Get in the car. I'm taking you home.'

Eve's heart, having skipped a beat somewhere, was now crashing about at twice its normal speed. Shocked into speechlessness, she shook her head in disbelief.

'I… You…' she spluttered. 'You are *unbelievable*! All of a sudden it's *my fault* for being in the way when *you* were driving like a complete madman in a pedestrian zone!'

Fists clenched into balls of frustration, Raphael cursed quietly and swung away while he regained his composure. When he turned back to address her his tone was grave, and without her glasses she completely missed the small, rueful smile that accompanied his words.

'Actually, it *was* your fault—yes.'

Eve saw red. '*Of course*! No—you're absolutely right! Naturally it was up to me to make sure I was not in the way of your testosterone-fuelled display of macho prowess. My fault entirely. But then I'm just a silly, inexperienced journalist on a low-rent publication,' she yelled, sarcastically echoing his words of that morning. 'It's completely over my little blonde head to walk safely along the street. I'm not fit—'

She didn't get any further. Without warning he reached out and slipped a hand beneath the silky fall of hair at the back of her neck and drew her mouth to his. The gentle pressure of his lips sent a surge of hot, liquid need crashing through her, driving out every logical thought and rational argument and replacing it with one thought, one desire.

Instinctively her body curved into his, and Luca's jacket slipped from her shoulders and fell to the ground. Raphael's tongue teased the sensitive softness of her mouth, and a small whimper of longing escaped her as his lips moved from hers to kiss the secret place beneath her ear.

She was lost, drowning in fathomless depths of ecstasy from which she had no wish ever to be rescued. Behind her closed eyelids the darkness swirled and formed itself into a thousand erotic images as the potent cocktail of four passionfruit daiquiris, one shot of adrenaline and a kick of one-hundred-percent pure longing went straight to her head. And her knees. And her…

His breath was warm against her neck as he murmured, 'Sorry. *I'm sorry*—OK? Come with me. Now.'

She heard him open the car door and her eyelids fluttered open, the daylight intruding starkly on her own dark world of fantasy. Raphael wasn't staring seductively into her eyes, but looking over her shoulder to where Luca still stood, watching them as he spoke quietly into his mobile phone.

'Come on. Into the car.'

Dumbly she slid into the low passenger seat and watched him stride grimly round to the other side of the car. The tenderness of a few moments before had evaporated, replaced by cold efficiency. A shiver ran through her as she realised the kiss had been nothing more than a tactic to get her into the car.

As he slipped sinuously into the driver's seat she swallowed nervously and shrank away from him, stunned by the change in him. God, what was she doing? How had she let herself be manipulated so easily? Her hand crept towards the door, but stopped before it reached the handle.

No. This was what she wanted.

She'd decided that she wasn't going back to England until she'd got the evidence she needed to convict him or clear him.

And she wasn't going to find that alone in a hotel room. She might not have exactly planned this little turn of events, but rum-fuelled logic and Dutch courage told her it was actually quite a stroke of luck.

Of course that was the reason she felt compelled to stay. It was nothing whatsoever to do with the fact that her fingers itched with the insane compulsion to touch the long, muscular thigh next to hers, to entwine themselves in his ruffled black hair, smoothing back the lock that fell over his face before…

Get over it! Biting her lip to prevent it trembling, she shrank further away from him, ashamed and afraid of the blatant longing that thrummed painfully inside her.

As he started the ignition with a deafening roar Raphael glanced sideways at her, taking in the quivering lip and huge, frightened eyes. A flash of irritation swept through him.

He was used to issuing orders and having them obeyed, but something had warned him that Eve Middlemiss would go out of her way to do the opposite of what she was told. Kissing her had been the only way of getting her into the car and away from Luca. He'd had no choice, he reassured himself.

So why did he feel like some kind of monster all of a sudden? Because he'd enjoyed kissing her? This was the twenty-first century—surely he could kiss someone without feeling as if he was guilty of some kind of violation? Especially when his motivation was purely her own good.

Purely? a little voice in his head taunted, forcing him to confront the reason for his guilt. Perhaps not. He had kissed her because he didn't have time to argue with her, and because standing there, with her green eyes flashing fire and brimstone, she had been almost impossible to resist. And that was the thing that irked him. He wanted her, and for a whole host of very good reasons he didn't *want* to want her.

Beside him, Eve surreptitiously checked in her bag. At least she had her phone. And her pink penknife.

It had been a birthday present from Lou: a joke, because it contained all the necessary tools for survival—a nail file, a miniature mirror, and most importantly a corkscrew. There was a blade on there too, but it remained stiff from lack of use— unlike the corkscrew—and Eve doubted whether she could get it out quickly enough in a moment of crisis. Oh, well, in that case she would just have to *screw* his brains out…

She let out a gurgle of laughter.

Raphael threw her a sharp glance.

'Something amusing?'

'Yes, I…' But the mental image, conjured by accident or Freudian design, wouldn't leave her. The laughter died on her lips as another wave of lust swept through her with the ruthless inevitability of a tidal-bore. She turned her face to look out of the window.

'Where are you staying?'

'Well, as of this afternoon, nowhere,' she muttered, trying to redirect her thoughts. 'I checked out of the hotel this morning.'

Raphael gritted his teeth. 'So what were you going to do?'

'Luca very kindly offered me a bed—no strings—and if it hadn't been for this stupid pretence that we're in—' She had been about to say *in love* but stumbled on the words and changed it at the last minute. 'Involved, I would be taking him up on it.'

No strings? Knowing Luca, it would be chains and handcuffs instead. How could she be so trusting? Exasperated, Raphael pushed his hair back from his forehead and shot her a sideways glance. Sitting with the glossy Lazaro goody bag clasped in her hands, twisting its silken rope handle around one slender finger, she looked incredibly young and frighteningly vulnerable. The thought of her on the streets or, much worse, in Luca's lair made him feel dizzy. He sucked in a breath and tried to keep his voice even.

'Stay with me.' It came out as a harsh rasp. What was the matter with him? He wouldn't blame her for refusing.

For a second she was very still, then she turned and gave him a small, brave smile.

'Really? Thanks.'

It was easy to see which of the narrow Florentine townhouses was Raphael's. It was the one with the crowd of paparazzi outside.

'Damn,' growled Raphael, accelerating past them. 'Quick. Get down.'

A shout went up from the pavement as one of the journalists spotted the car and gave chase. Eve caught a fleeting glimpse of the blonde from the press conference before Raphael's hand clasped the back of her neck and pulled her head down.

Her cheek was pressed against the hardness of his thigh, and she could feel his muscles flexing as he changed up a gear. His arm covered her, the scent of him filled her head, and the world outside the window was upside down.

'Wh-what are you doing?'

'Unless you want your picture all over the gossip columns, stay there,' he hissed. 'We have some bloody fool on a motorbike following us.'

She closed her eyes and breathed him in, feeling oddly safe and protected, like when she was a child and she and Ellie would curl up together on the back seat on the way back from some concert or gala performance in which their mother had been singing. The denim beneath her cheek had been washed to faded softness, and it smelled clean and comforting, and the rocking motion of the car as Raphael wove expertly through the backstreets soothed her. Really, that passionfruit whatever had been very nice, but it had made her feel quite sleepy…

Negotiating a labyrinthine path through the ancient narrow streets around the Piazza della Signoria, Raphael tried to keep his mind on the paparazzo motorcyclist and off the tousled golden head in his lap.

Impossible.

He could feel the warmth of her breath against his thigh, in a place where the caress of a woman's breath should mean one thing and one thing only…

Don't go there! Gripping the steering wheel, he cast around desperately for something deeply boring and unerotic to think about, to counter the inevitable effect she was having on him. Railway timetables. Exchange rates. International time zones.

Just when he feared his self-control might snap, he realised the motorcyclist was no longer on his tail. Glancing round to make sure he was nowhere to be seen, Raphael let out an exhalation of relief.

'It's OK—you can get up now.'

She shifted slightly, bringing her hand up to her face and letting it come to rest on his knee, the fingers curling delicately upwards. Hardly daring to breathe, Raphael gently brushed the hair off her face, knowing already what he would find.

Dark lashes swept down over flushed cheeks, mouth pressed into a perfect cupid's bow—she was asleep.

A sharp kick of desire knocked the air from his lungs and an involuntary moan from his lips. The traffic in front of him slowed to a near standstill and, waiting in the queue, he took both hands off the steering wheel and thrust them savagely through his hair, as if in an effort to prevent himself from touching her.

She looked like a child, she behaved like a rebellious teenager, she exasperated him beyond measure and she was causing him an inordinate amount of trouble. But at that moment he wanted Eve Middlemiss so much he couldn't think straight.

She awoke as he turned the engine off. Struggling to sit up, she widened her eyes with horror as she realised where she was.

'Oh…oh, no…What did I…?'

Raphael's face was completely expressionless. 'You fell asleep.'

She gave a little moan of distress. 'Sorry. I can't think what came over me.'

'I can,' he said sardonically. 'At least four disgusting rum-based cocktails, courtesy of my dear half-brother.'

'Rum?' she whimpered. 'But he said they were almost non-alcoholic!'

'That figures,' said Raphael bitterly, getting out of the car.

Eve followed. 'Where are we?' she asked, looking up at the imposing façade of the building with a mixture of anxiety and awe. Four storeys of mellow golden stone towered above her, graced by delicate wrought-iron balconies at the long first- and second-floor windows. A double flight of stone steps led to the front door.

'My father's house,' he replied curtly.

'Won't he mind?' Eve followed him, trying not to gaze too hungrily on the broad shoulders beneath the cornflower-blue linen shirt. She still felt slow with sleep, and dazed by conflicting emotions. If he was a potential drug-pushing sadist, why did she just want to curl up on his knee again?

Over his shoulder, he shot her a stony look. 'I realise that the finer points of this morning's press conference may have gone over your head, Eve, but I thought that even you had managed to follow the general gist. Antonio is in hospital. But,' he continued, opening the door into a beautifully proportioned domed hallway, 'he has a housekeeper who will be only too glad to have someone to fuss over while he is away.'

Eve stopped in the middle of the shining marble floor and looked around her. It was like stepping onto the set of one of the glamorous 1950s movies her mother had loved so much. In front of her a staircase with an ornately embellished wrought-iron balustrade rose to a gallery above, and on the ceiling cherubs cavorted around ample-figured goddesses holding strategically-placed garlands.

She was so busy taking it all in that at first she didn't notice a stout woman with greying hair scraped into a bun appear in the doorway at the end of the hall.

'Raphael!'

'*Ciao*, Fiora. *Come stai?*'

He stepped forward to embrace her, and they talked in rapid Italian for a minute or two before Eve became aware that they had both turned to look at her. Raphael switched back into English for her benefit.

'Eve, this is Fiora—my father's invaluable, irreplaceable housekeeper.'

Eve smiled shyly under the older woman's curious scrutiny, and wondered what Raphael had said about her.

'Fiora doesn't speak much English, I'm afraid, but I'm sure the two of you will manage to get along.' Picking up his keys from a marble-topped console table, he began to walk back towards the door.

Eve was assailed by sudden panic. He couldn't mean to just leave her here—could he?

'Raphael…'

He turned, one dark eyebrow raised in silent question as his eyes met hers. She wanted to run to him and feel the reassuring strength of his arms around her, to beg him not to leave her, to take her with him, but she was rooted to the spot and the words wouldn't come.

'Don't go,' she managed huskily, feeling a deep blush suffuse her cheeks.

For a second she thought she saw the ghost of a smile at the corner of his mouth before he turned away and strode towards the door.

'I'm just going to collect your things from the hotel,' he said. 'I'm sure you'll be OK with Fiora for half an hour.'

Scarlet with humiliation, Eve followed Fiora up the wide staircase.

CHAPTER FIVE

WHERE on earth had that come from?

Trailing despondently behind Fiora, Eve gritted her teeth and kept her eyes fixed on the floor. *Don't go...*she heard herself saying, the words sounding pathetically girly and weak as they echoed around her head. What the hell had come over her? The man had just virtually kidnapped her, and she was practically falling over herself to thank him. It would be funny if it wasn't quite so appalling.

Well, one thing was certain. She wouldn't be caught off guard again.

Make that two things. She wouldn't be touching another passionfruit daiquiri any time soon either.

Fiora came to a halt outside one of the doors along the impossibly grand corridor and pushed it open, standing aside to let Eve go through.

Entering hesitantly, she had to stop herself from gasping out loud.

The room was like something out of a fairy tale. In its centre stood a huge bed, dressed in beautiful vintage linen and topped with an antique gilded corona from which acres of white muslin were romantically draped. A small sofa and two dainty chairs upholstered in soft duck-egg blue linen were arranged around a low table on which a tray with a coffee pot and two elegant china espresso cups were laid.

It made the plush hotel she'd been staying in look like a youth hostel.

Resisting the urge to throw herself onto the bed and nestle into the pile of silk cushions Eve walked over to one of the floor-length windows and found herself looking out over a walled garden at the back of the villa. The windows opened onto a small terrace, from which one could enjoy the delicate fragrance of lilies and orange blossom that drifted up from the terraced garden below.

Behind her, humming quietly, Fiora bustled about, plumping up pillows and carefully moving some of the silk cushions. Then she disappeared into an adjoining room, which Eve guessed was an *en-suite* bathroom. A moment later she heard the sound of running water.

Returning to collect an armful of thick, snowy towels from the armoire, Fiora caught sight of Eve's bewildered expression. The humming stopped and her face creased into lines of kindness.

'*Bagno*… Bath?'

'Thank you, but…'

'Signor Raphael—he say you…*molto stanco*…?'

Eve gave a little cry of fury. 'How dare he? Anyway,' she muttered sulkily, 'it's not my fault. It's that horrible perfume from the launch.'

Fiora looked shocked, then upset. 'Sorry, *signorina…molto stanco*…how you say?' She put her head to one side and closed her eyes.

'Asleep?' suggested Eve doubtfully.

'*Si!* He say you very sleepy! He say you rest, but I think maybe after *bagno* you feel better?'

Feeling suddenly foolish and ungrateful, Eve managed a smile. 'Yes. Thank you, Fiora. You are very kind.'

Fiora dismissed her words with a wave of her hand. '*Per niente. A dopo, signorina.*'

When the door had closed quietly behind her, Eve pressed her burning cheek against the cool windowpane. The temptation to climb down the balcony and escape over the garden wall was suddenly pretty strong.

OK, so—as any one of her friends would testify—she was hardly a winner in the ice-cool grace and sophistication stakes, but she wasn't usually so totally inept. What was it about Raphael Di Lazaro that had turned her into a dizzy blonde with an IQ lower than her bra size and a head full of marshmallow?

She had a degree from a top British university, for crying out loud, a good job and a clean driving licence. And yet in the twenty-four hours since she'd laid eyes on Raphael di Lazaro she had been behaving like a gawky schoolgirl on her first foreign exchange visit.

If she couldn't snap out of it and take control of the situation she might as well go home now.

The fact that he was horribly attractive was inconvenient, but she was an intelligent and mature woman, and it wasn't as if she'd never seen a good-looking male before. Admittedly the Department of Renaissance Poetry wasn't exactly heaving with them, but that was no excuse for dissolving into a puddle of hormones every time Raphael Di Lazaro glanced at her.

No. The problem wasn't what he looked like, it was the man himself.

Last night when he had kissed her she had had a tantalising insight into what she believed was the real man beneath that iron self-control and breathtaking arrogance. And the real Raphael wasn't anything like the monster she had come here expecting to find.

Suddenly the spark of an idea flickered into life in her head, momentarily illuminating her gloomy thoughts. Reflected in the glass of the windowpane her eyes were wide and dark as her mind raced over the plan that was forming there.

If she was going to find out whether he was capable of the

*crime she suspected him of, she needed to see that side of him
again. More closely. Flirt with him. Seduce him. Peel away the
layers until the man she had glimpsed last night was naked
before her. Then she'd see who he really was.*

She wandered thoughtfully over to her bag and slipped a little
photograph of herself and Ellie out of her purse. In it she was
sitting down, a small smile on her face. Ellie stood behind her,
her arms wrapped around Eve's shoulders, her head thrown back
in laughter. Looking at it now, what struck Eve more forcefully
than ever before was not how similar they looked, but how different had been their whole approach to life. She had always
prided herself on her sense and steadiness, disapproving of Ellie's
total abandonment and limitless capacity for fun. Suddenly she
saw how blinkered she'd been, and deep inside her she felt the stir-
rings of anticipation. It was time to live a little more dangerously.

Operation Seduction started here. Make or break.

A shiver rippled through her and she realised that for the first
time since she had left England she was properly frightened.

Partly because of what she might find.

But mainly because of what she might lose in the process.

Raphael put down the bag and hesitated before knocking quietly
on the door to Eve's room.

He had intended to ask Fiora to bring Eve's things up to her,
but had found her up to her elbows in flour in the kitchen. Had
he imagined the twinkle in her dark eyes as she had given him
a tall glass of iced elderflower cordial to take up to Eve, along
with instructions to tell her that dinner was almost ready?

It would have been petty and ungracious to refuse. He had
brought Eve here, after all.

He pressed his ear to the heavy wood and knocked again. This
time, very faintly, he heard Eve call out—something which he
couldn't be sure was 'come in', but definitely wasn't angry
enough to be 'go away'—or worse.

Entering her room, he was immediately hit by the delicate, dizzying floral scent of Lazaro perfume. The concealed sound system was playing the bit from *Madame Butterfly* to which Eve had walked down the runway at the retrospective, but the room was empty.

From through the open door of the bathroom came the unmistakable trickle of water.

She was in the bath.

Closing her eyes, Eve sank back beneath the bubbles and felt all the stress of the day evaporate.

The first stars were beginning to appear in the hazy violet sky thorough the open French doors, but not a breath of wind disturbed the steadily burning candles in the deliciously over-the-top gothic-style candelabras that flanked them.

With a deep roll-top bath in the centre of the floor, it was easily the most stunning bathroom she had ever seen, and discovering the remote controlled stereo system built into one of the cupboards in the bedroom—complete with extensive CD collection—had been the double-chocolate-fudge icing on the cake.

From where she lay, chin-deep in scented bubbles, she had the whole of Florence laid out before her. She could see the dome of the Duomo, the closely packed terracotta-tiled rooftops of the narrow streets, the twinkling lights of the *piazzas*. Swinging a dripping foot over the side of the bath, she let the beauty of the music and the perfection of the setting work their magic.

Her limbs felt warm and languid from the heat of the water, and a pulse beat insistently at the top of her thighs at the prospect of what she was planning to do. Letting the exquisite notes pour over her, she added her voice to that of Butterfly, remembering as she did so the feeling of Raphael's eyes upon her as she swayed down the catwalk towards him. Her whole body throbbed. Closing her eyes, she let her head fall back against the rim of the bathtub, abandoning herself completely to the music. Arching her dripping arms above her head, she sang with all her heart.

Raphael hesitated. He should leave.

Obviously.

But…

He found himself drawn forward. The hairs on the back of his neck rose as her voice drifted out across the scented air. Unselfconsciously sweet and true, it soared effortlessly up to the highest notes, the acoustics of the bathroom giving it an even more flattering resonance.

And she knew the words, he realised with surprise.

He stopped when he reached the doorway. Through the half-open door, in the candlelit dusk, he could see one glistening brown leg draped enticingly over the side of the bath. He swallowed, somehow managing to stop himself from going further into the room, but unable to prevent his imagination from generating the images of what he would see if he did.

He cleared his throat, both to draw attention to his presence and to clear the sudden constriction there that seemed to be making it difficult to breathe.

A tidal wave of foam cascaded over the sides of the bath as Eve let out a squeal of alarm and slipped down until her chin was level with the surface of the water.

'How long have you been there?' she gasped.

'Long enough to be impressed. You have a beautiful voice. And it seems I was wrong—you do speak Italian after all.'

'Not really,' Eve replied shakily. 'I just know some of the words from *Butterfly*, which somehow never seem to come up in general conversation. Anyway,' she continued, her outrage increasing as her fear subsided, 'was there a good reason for you to sneak into my room uninvited? Or did you just want to frighten the living daylights out of me?'

'I knocked. I thought I heard you say come in. Fiora sent a drink up for you.' He rattled the ice cubes in the glass. 'And she asked me to tell you that dinner will be in half an hour, if you'd care to get dressed.'

'Dressing for dinner?' Eve had a sudden vision of herself and Raphael in evening wear, sitting at opposite ends of a long, polished mahogany table while Fiora waited on them. 'Are you always so formal?'

'I didn't mean it like that. I simply meant as opposed to eating naked.'

His tone was light and mocking. The music had finished, and for a moment the silence spread around them like a dark pool. She was glad the open door stood between them, so he couldn't see the deep blush that was rising from her cleavage to her cheeks at the thought of sharing a meal with him…naked.

She took a steadying breath. 'Not a good idea,' she said as lightly as possible. 'Especially if soup is on the menu.'

'It so happens that it isn't tonight…' He paused for a heartbeat. 'But even so… I'll expect you in half an hour.'

Knickers. So much for Operation Seduction. Not only had he caught her completely off guard, and rather scuppered her intention to appear mysterious and sophisticated, he'd also totally shattered the atmosphere of tranquil relaxation. Hauling herself up crossly, Eve let the water cascade off her body before stepping out of the bath and looking round for a towel.

'Damn, damn, *damn!*'

Still dripping wet, and starting to shiver slightly in the breeze from the open windows, she headed for the bedroom, where the pile of towels still lay on the bed as Fiora had left them. Dusk had fallen properly now, and the only light in the bathroom came from the candles. The rest of the room was filled with shadow. Eve was halfway across the polished floor when she caught sight of herself in the huge and ornately carved mirror.

She stopped, suddenly overtaken by insecurity. The plan was ridiculous anyway. There was no way an inhibited, pitifully inexperienced girl like her would ever be able to seduce a man like Raphael Di Lazaro. Was there?

Slowly she faced the mirror, experimentally pulling in her stomach and thrusting out her breasts, then lasciviously sweeping her hair up off her neck and holding it loosely on top of her head. Her cheeks were flushed from the heat of the bath, and the candlelight cast a glow onto her skin, lending a golden voluptuousness to her generous breasts and softly rounded hips, and throwing flattering shadows beneath her cheekbones and ribs. Crystal droplets of water still glittered on her arms and throat, and ran in slow, caressing rivulets between her breasts and down her thighs.

'You'll be needing this.'

Raphael's voice from the doorway made her start. Holding out one of the sumptuous towels, he moved towards her, his expression unsmiling, his eyes hooded and unreadable.

'Thank you. I can…'

In a trance, she watched in the mirror as deftly he wrapped the towel around her. In the candlelight and against the snowy whiteness of the towel his forearms were dark, dark brown. His movements were firm and capable as he rubbed her upper arms through the thick fabric, and her protestations died on her lips as she meekly submitted to his ministrations. Half in a dream she noticed that her eyes glittered with desire and her lips were plump and parted. She ran her tongue over them.

She stumbled slightly as he abruptly let her go.

'There. Now, do you think you can manage to get dressed by yourself, or shall I send Fiora up?'

His voice was cool and faintly sardonic. Eve's chin rose a fraction in shock and defiance as she registered his indifference. Pulling the towel more tightly around herself, she swept out of the bathroom with as much dignity as she could muster, resisting the urge to slam the door behind her.

* * *

As he impatiently began to extinguish the candles Raphael was painfully aware of the ironic symbolism of the gesture.

If only the burn of his own desire could be so easily snuffed out.

It was a mistake to have brought Eve here. He should have paid for her to stay at the hotel for another night, having persuaded her to book onto a London flight tomorrow morning. Not that it would be easy to persuade Eve to do anything, but her friend to whom he had spoken on the phone that morning could be a possible ally—

At exactly that moment, almost as if he had made it happen himself, he heard the faint ring of a mobile phone above the sound of water draining noisily from the bath. In the semi-darkness it wasn't difficult to spot the greenish glow of its screen on the marble-topped washstand, and he picked it up, wondering if it might be the same girl.

A quiet curse escaped his lips as he recognised the number on the screen.

Luca.

No. He had had no choice but to keep Eve with him, he realised grimly as he slipped the phone into his pocket. Whatever it was that she knew, Luca was onto her, and he would go to any lengths to shut her up. Two years ago he had let his pride prevent him from protecting Catalina. He would not make the same mistake again.

Besides which, she wasn't to be trusted! Irritation prickled through him at the thought that she had almost succeeded in making him forget the small detail of her profession and her purpose for being here. *She was a journalist.*

From now until Luca was safely in police custody he was not letting Eve Middlemiss leave his side. No matter how miserable that was for both of them.

For the briefest moment he caught a glimpse of his reflection in the mirror as he bent to blow out the last candle. His habitual blank sardonic mask had slipped, and he was jolted by the raw emotion that burned in the dark hollows of his eyes.

Swiftly, ruthlessly, he blew out the delicate flame and the image was gone.

But the unwelcome memory remained.

CHAPTER SIX

THE hallway was shadowed and silent as Eve came slowly down the stairs twenty minutes later. Beneath the thin silk of her dress she could feel her heart hammering wildly at the terrifying, exciting prospect of what she was about to do.

Never before had she deliberately, wantonly, set out to seduce someone, and thinking about it like that the idea horrified her.

But she was shamefully aware that it aroused her a whole lot more.

Crossing the marble-tiled hallway towards the lighted doorway of the salon, she pressed her glossed lips together nervously and smoothed the slippery silk of her dress over her hips. It was the same dress she'd worn for the retrospective party, and the only remotely sexy thing she'd brought with her. Despite the stifling heat of the evening she'd added a sumptuously wide pashmina in soft olive-green, which brought out the colour of her eyes. And, more importantly, concealed the tell-tale outline of her nipples which, after her encounter with Raphael in the bathroom, had refused to play along with her brain in pretending that she was entirely in control of the situation.

If she was going to try to seduce him she would do it with a degree of dignity. Not offer herself up on a plate.

The salon was softly lit by lamps, and the scent of gardenia and roses flooded through the open doors beyond which Eve could see the glint of candlelight on crystal. She was trembling as she crossed the room, and her little jeweled sandals made no sound on the polished parquet.

In the doorway, she hesitated. On the terrace a table was beautifully laid with white linen and heavy silver cutlery, and a huge bowl of pink and apricot roses were shedding their velvet petals onto the snowy damask. A large and ornate silver candelabra provided the centrepiece and cast its soft light into the violet dusk.

Raphael's head was bent over a newspaper, a slight frown of concentration furrowing his forehead beneath the lock of wayward hair that habitually fell across it. As Eve watched he swept it back impatiently with lean, tanned fingers. The gesture was utterly unselfconscious, but powerfully, exquisitely sexy.

She wasn't aware of making any sound, but she must have because he looked up sharply. His expression didn't change at all, but neither did his eyes leave her as he slowly rose and pulled out her chair.

'I see you did dress, after all.'

Gratefully she sat down, suddenly afraid that her knees might give way beneath her. There was something very intimate about the beautiful candlelit terrace in the warm evening, and it seemed to change the atmosphere, charging it with some invisible electric force that crackled between them like late-summer thunder on the distant hills.

'Yes.'

He took a bottle of prosecco from the ice bucket and poured it into two slender flutes. 'As you can see, Fiora doesn't do low-key catering.' His mouth twisted into a sardonic smile. 'In this case she seems to have slightly misread the situation.'

She took the glass he offered, trying not to jump as her fingers brushed against his.

'It's beautiful.'

He looked around, as if noticing for the first time. 'It is.

Beautiful, but oppressive.' He gave a short, humourless laugh. 'Welcome to the world of Lazaro. Appearances are everything.'

'Did you grow up here?'

'Yes.'

Her eyes met his over the rim of her glass. She took a slow sip of wine, intrigued by the image of Raphael as a little boy in these vast, formal rooms. Suddenly his emotional inscrutability and hauteur seemed more understandable.

'What was it like? I can't imagine it was a house where children would feel very comfortable. Did you and Luca have a wild time, sliding down the banisters and getting told off for driving your toy cars over the antique furniture?'

She spoke lightly, trying not to notice the way the candlelight emphasised the hollows beneath his cheekbones and the deep shadows of fatigue around his eyes. By contrast, his voice was like gravel.

'Not exactly. Luca and I may be brothers—half-brothers, to be more precise—but we barely know each other.'

'And can barely stand each other, either?'

He grimaced. 'How did you guess?'

She paused, running her fingers slowly up and down the stem of her champagne flute and trying to focus on what he was saying, rather than the electric current coursing around her pelvis. 'Oh, let me see… Could it have been the less than affectionate way you greeted him at the retrospective party, and then again today? On both occasions I got the distinct impression that you were more likely to smash his face in than shake his hand.'

He gave her a wry smile. 'Was it that obvious?'

'I'm afraid so. Even to someone as "silly and inexperienced" as me.' She looked up at him through lowered lashes and smiled teasingly. 'Even to someone as *blind* and silly and inexperienced as me. What I still haven't worked out is why.'

Given that she had to be the world's least experienced flirt, she was taking to it with worrying ease. But flirting with Raphael was as easy as breathing. It was something about the way he moved his long-fingered hands as he spoke, and the triangle of sun-bronzed skin at the open collar of his blue shirt, and his mouth...

What wasn't so easy was remembering that this was just a manoeuvre in a game. She was playing a part, that was all. Cynically acting out a role as a means to an end. The thought made her feel as uncomfortable as the throbbing ache between her thighs.

'Why what?'

With a fingertip, Eve chased a bead of condensation down the side of her glass. She found herself unable to look at him, but was aware of his eyes following every movement.

'Why you hate him so much that you had to lie to him about us being together. Was it just to make sure he didn't get something that you hadn't got, regardless of whether you really wanted it?'

'Who said I didn't want it?' he said softly.

She was spared the need to answer because at that moment Fiora arrived, carrying a tray laden with food. Which was just as well because Eve couldn't have spoken anyway. The charge in the air between her and Raphael could have lit an entire city.

Fiora placed a bowl of salad and a basket of warm, fragrant bread on the table, then laid a plate of delicately scented risotto topped with asparagus spears drizzled with olive oil before each of them. Picking up on the taut lines of tension, she beamed knowingly and hurried away.

Eve picked up one of the slender spears and captured its tip between her lips. It was delicious—the essence of hot Italian summer concentrated into one distinctive taste—and she closed her eyes to savour it, realising how hungry she was. When she opened them again it was to find Raphael leaning back in his chair and watching her intently, his face shadowed and unreadable.

Colour flooded her cheeks as she sucked the fragrant oil off her fingers. She felt dizzy. Her pashmina had slipped off her shoulders, and she was painfully aware that her nipples were jutting against the silk of her dress.

She looked down, picking up one of the fallen rose petals and smoothing its bruised surface with her fingers. It felt like damp flesh. Memories of his hands on her body in the bathroom only an hour ago came back to her in a rush of heat.

It was as if he had read her mind.

'So it seems, Signorina Middlemiss, that you're something of a dark horse. Where did that exceptional singing voice come from?'

'My mother was a singer. A soprano. My sister and I spent our childhoods traipsing around from one concert to the next, sleeping in dressing rooms and doing our homework in the orchestra pit during rehearsals.'

Raphael raised an eyebrow. 'Your father?'

'First violin.' She paused. 'Apparently.'

'You never knew him?'

His voice was gentle, and she found herself not wanting to meet his eyes. It was impossible to hate him when he spoke to her like that.

'No.'

Her answer hung in the air for a moment before the silence swallowed it.

'Lucky you,' he said drily. 'I often find myself wishing I could say the same.'

She gave him a brief smile, grateful in spite of herself that he had been sensitive enough to realise she didn't want to talk about it. 'How is your father? Have you had any news from the hospital?'

'No change. It seems his heart is in pretty bad shape. Though I must say I'm surprised that he has one at all. I never saw much evidence of it when I was growing up.'

'What about your mother? Were you close to her?'

He was suddenly very still. 'Yes. She died when I was seven…'

'Oh, Raphael…' The small intimacy escaped her lips in a whispered caress before she could stop it. If he noticed he didn't show it.

Laying down his fork, he leaned back in his chair and continued. 'My father remarried almost straight away. I was something of a thorn in the side of his new wife, so by the time Luca came along I was safely incarcerated in an English boarding school. Hence our lack of brotherly devotion.'

His voice was low and faintly sardonic, but the pain behind his words wasn't difficult to detect. Her foolish, traitorous heart went out to him.

'And your impeccable English.'

'I had to learn pretty quickly. Not that most of the first words I picked up are suitable for repetition over the dinner table. Pretty Italian boys were something of a novelty.'

'I bet you were pretty, too.' She spoke almost without thinking, then blushed. 'I don't mean… It's just, with your bone structure and colouring…' She looked down at her plate, continuing in a breathless rush. 'My sister and I always longed to go to boarding school. It sounded like heaven to us. Were you happy there?'

'No. It was hell.' Picking up a roll, he tore into it with long, savage fingers. 'After being used to all this, I hated the greyness and the cold. My father wasn't the best correspondent—too absorbed with his new family.' He said the words as if they tasted bitter in his mouth. 'And I suppose I hadn't got over my mother's death.'

'Of course you hadn't! You were just a little boy. Even with the love and understanding of your father it would have been impossible to get over something like that.'

Pouring more prosecco into her glass, he gave a dry laugh. 'You're quite right. Unfortunately, in the absence of love and understanding from my father, I grew up into a bitter, twisted and emotionally bankrupt—'

'Don't say that.'

The words came from her in something halfway between a whisper and a moan. It was as though she couldn't bear to hear him say the things her head suspected to be true and which her heart was so fervently trying to deny. He stopped abruptly and passed a hand over his face. In the velvety quiet of the twilight Eve heard the slight rasp of his unshaven skin.

He was very still, but his eyes burned into hers through the darkness. For a moment neither of them moved. This was her moment—the perfect chance to put her plan into action—but that wasn't what she was thinking as she got up and moved slowly round the table towards him.

She wasn't thinking at all, but acting on pure, primitive instinct.

Her bare arm brushed against the bowl of roses, sending a ripple of anticipation over her exquisitely sensitised skin and a cascade of petals onto the table. Their scent filled the warm air as she reached him: heavy, sensual, intoxicating. As if in a trance she reached out and pressed her palm against his cheek. His gaze didn't flicker, but remained locked onto hers, intense and unfathomable. And then his fingers closed over her hand, pulling her down towards him until her mouth met his.

It was like dying and being reborn. Adrenalin, desire, and ten thousand volts of sexual electricity crashed through her as her parted lips were crushed against his in the savagery of their need. She was dimly aware of moving, so that she was standing over him, straddling him where he sat, but it was as if she was under the control of a higher being, unconsciously obeying an imperative that she neither questioned nor understood. All she knew was that the sensation of his hands—in her hair, caressing her back, moving downwards to the firm curve of her buttocks—was the most unimaginably erotic thing she had ever experienced.

She shifted her position so that she was sitting on his knee, astride him, the thin silk of her narrow slip dress riding up over her parted thighs. His hands found the warm skin, his thumbs making caressing circles on her quivering flesh as their mouths continued their urgent, savage quest.

He made a low sound deep in his throat, a guttural growl of longing, and then tore his lips from hers.

She was aware of his fingers closing like bracelets of steel around her wrists, pulling her hands away from his face. Bewildered, bereft, she got to her feet, pressing the back of her hand against her swollen lips.

'Wh—what..?

Raphael barely glanced at her. His face was like granite.

'Fiora.'

Eve whirled around as Fiora bustled out onto the terrace. The older woman's small eyes were wide and knowing, and she set about clearing the table with great focus, trying to conceal the broad smile that she couldn't quite suppress.

'Here—let me help.'

Eve sprang forward, needing to do something to prevent herself from having to see the look of dark despair on Raphael's face. As she helped Fiora gather the remains of their meal and carry it through to the kitchen her mind was racing, along with her pulse.

It was what she had planned. So why did it feel as if she'd been run over by an express train?

And why did she want to lie right back down on the track and be run over again?

After they'd gone Raphael drew a deep, ragged breath and buried his face in his hands.

He should go and help. He knew that. But first he had to wait for the hard, throbbing evidence of his desire to subside.

Picking up his wine glass, he drained it in one long mouthful and slumped back in his chair. Fiora's appearance had been entirely coincidental. He had been trying to break off the kiss anyway, trying to exercise some form of restraint from where he would make an attempt to find the right words to tell her what they were doing was impossible.

For a few moments there he had been totally out of control, and that was something he found very hard to accept. What in hell's name had possessed him? Never before had he spoken to anyone about those things. What on earth had made him spill out all the tawdry details of his miserable childhood like some spineless, self-pitying wimp?

Being back in this house. Too many memories. Too much unhappiness and resentment. That was all it was.

And yet he'd brought other women here over the years, and none of them had ever seen the pain that lurked in the corner of each beautiful room, nor smelt the loneliness that hung like a mist over the lavish furnishings. Not a single one of those clever, ambitious, sophisticated women had ever suspected that to Raphael this villa was anything other than a comfortable family home. Catalina, the woman he had almost married, certainly hadn't.

Eve had.

But he shouldn't confuse her listening skills with anything else, for pity's sake. She had a knack, it was true, of putting her head slightly to one side when you were speaking, as if she was hanging on your every word, and her turquoise eyes seemed to shine with compassion. But she was a journalist, *per l'amore di Dio*. Using Feminine Wiles to Extract Information was probably one of the training modules she'd completed at college. With distinction.

Maybe she was smarter than she looked. Maybe that blonde softness and the sleepy, seductive look in those clear greenish eyes was carefully cultivated. Maybe that kiss was all part of the act and had nothing to do with love…

He made a sharp noise of self-disgust. Of course it was an act. *Love?* What the hell had make him think of that? It was a word he had banished from his vocabulary and his emotional repertoire years ago—probably about the time that Catalina had accused him of being incapable of it.

He hadn't bothered to argue with her. She'd been right. He'd never really loved her. Wanted her, yes, and enjoyed her athletic model's body and the textbook sex that had made up their relationship, but she'd never really got beneath his skin in that visceral, all-consuming, irrational way that to him meant love.

He frowned as the knife of guilt twisted in that old wound. It hadn't occurred to him that she hadn't felt like that too until she'd left with Luca, and he had to live with the knowledge of what had happened to her as a result every day. But he'd learned from it, and he had vowed never to risk causing such pain to anyone again.

And that included Eve Middlemiss.

She was just a kid—twenty-one or twenty-two at the most. He had brought her here to protect her, not take advantage of her. One destroyed life on his conscience was bad enough. No matter what she did for a living, he would not risk screwing Eve up too.

Cursing quietly, he dropped his head into his hands. It hardly mattered what the truth was.

Either way, from now on she was strictly off limits.

After the muggy heat of the kitchen the warm evening air was like a caress on her skin, and Eve took a deep steadying breath of it as she stepped back onto the terrace. The two tiny cups of espresso she carried rattled slightly in her trembling hands.

The kitchen was immaculate, and Fiora had made sure all the lights downstairs, except the lamps in the salon, were put out before she had agreed to retire to her room. Assuring her that they would take care of everything else, Eve had said goodnight and watched her stiffly climb the back stairs.

Her mind was in turmoil. This was it.

She stopped, feeling the sweat break out on her forehead. The pulse between her legs was like a raw, primitive drumbeat, echoing the pounding blood in her ears. She was bewitched by its insistent rhythm, like the girl with the red shoes in the fairy tale, unable to stop her body from responding, increasingly ter-rified by the strength of that response. Maybe it was some primeval instinct for self-preservation that at that moment wouldn't allow her to make the connection between Ellie's death and the man she was about to approach...

Maybe it was just pure, old-fashioned, selfish lust.

Trembling violently, she bit down on her lip, assailed by doubt. What if he rejected her? She steeled herself, remember-ing the chilling moment at the press conference, when she had met his eyes and found only distaste.

But she couldn't turn back now. Not for Ellie. Not for herself.

She walked tentatively towards the table. He was leaning back in his chair, his long legs outstretched. As she came closer and saw his face she realised that he was asleep.

One arm was thrown across his body while the other sup-ported his head, and in spite of the obvious discomfort of his position he looked peaceful. Sleep had softened his features and smoothed away the harsh lines of bitterness and cynicism.

God, he was perfect.

Crushing disappointment fought with an acute sense of frus-tration as she kneeled beside him and gently she took hold of his hand.

'Raphael?'

He didn't stir. Holding his hand, she gave it a little shake, and he turned his head a fraction so that the light from the salon fell onto the high arc of one cheekbone and gilded the dark crescent of his eyelashes. Then he was perfectly still again.

Hardly daring to breathe, she turned his hand over.

The sleeve of his shirt was rolled back, and gingerly she eased it up a little further. Heart hammering, her eyes swept over the underside of his arm. It was a smooth, uniform butterscotch-brown.

There was no sign of the cruel black scars of drug abuse that had marred Ellie's arms when Eve had seen her in the hospital morgue.

She closed her eyes for a second and exhaled slowly, shutting the lid on the image that haunted her nightmares. Gently replacing his hand, she felt almost light-headed with relief, and had to check herself firmly. Just because he showed no signs of addiction himself, it didn't mean he couldn't be a supplier.

But that was unlikely, wasn't it?

The heat was gradually ebbing out of the evening, and Eve suddenly realised that she was shivering. She hesitated, unsure whether to wake him. Bending down, she put her lips to his ear and whispered.

'Raphael.'

The faint lemon and sandalwood scent of his skin knocked the air from her lungs and sent a surge of honeyed heat rushing through her. She could just discern the beat of his pulse beneath the skin of his neck, and it took every ounce of self-control she possessed to stop herself reaching forward and brushing her lips against it.

She stood up quickly, stealing an anxious glance at his face. He was still far away in the darkest depths of an exhausted sleep, but a faint smile lifted the corners of his mouth. Taking off her pashmina, she draped it over him, then stepped back hastily, suddenly too tired and confused to ask herself why she should want to look after this man.

Picking up the cups of cooling coffee, she had turned to go back into the house when the ring of a mobile phone stopped her in her tracks.

Her first thought was that it was *her* phone, and she should silence it before it woke him.

Her second thought was that she didn't have her phone on her.

The little silk shift had no room for the kind of pocket that would accommodate a mobile phone, and she hadn't brought a bag down with her—so where the hell was it?

Swiftly she replaced the cups on the table and followed the sound. It was coming from Raphael's direction—maybe he had the same phone she did? Leaning over him, she slipped her hands into both front pockets of his jeans.

Nothing.

The ringing continued. To get her hands in his back pockets she had to adopt pretty much the same position as she had done just half an hour earlier. Steeling herself to ignore the butterfly kiss of his breath against her breasts, she managed to reach round him without waking him. Just when she thought her self-control might snap she felt her fingers close around the phone. Gently she extracted it.

It was her phone.

Typically, at that moment the ringing stopped, and Eve was left in the sudden silence feeling more alone than she ever had in her life.

In the safety of her room she threw herself down onto the bed without even bothering to switch on a light, and called Lou back.

'Eve! I was about to file you as a missing person! What's going on?'

'It was my phone that was missing, not me. Although I am beginning to feel completely and utterly lost.'

That summed the situation up pretty well. Lost as in alone in a strange house in a foreign country. Lost as in uncertain of what was going on. Lost as in unrecognisable to herself. The Eve Middlemiss she knew didn't leave her seat at the dinner table to climb on top of the man opposite and eat his face rather than dessert.

'Let's start with the basics, then. Where are you?'

Eve sighed. 'Paradise. Antonio Di Lazaro's villa, just outside Florence.'

'With?'

'Raphael.'

There was a long silence on the other end of the line. When Lou eventually spoke her voice was sharp with anguish.

'Do you want me to call the police now, or would you rather wait until he actually has his hands around your throat and a gun to your head?'

Eve squeezed her eyes shut and massaged her forehead. '*Don't*, Lou. It's not like that. Honestly, I'm not in any danger.' *Except from my own rampaging emotions.*

'How do you know that?'

Eve sighed. 'I just do. I feel safe.'

Lou let out a shriek of disbelief. 'Oh, I see! Well, that's OK then, is it? *You feel safe!* That's the most ridiculous thing I've heard since…well, since this morning, when you came out with that line about Raphael Di Lazaro "having a strength about him". Honestly, what's the matter with you? Has he brainwashed you, or something? Is he there now, with a gun trained on you?'

'No,' she said in a small, cold voice. 'Look, Lou, I know it sounds crazy and I'm not sure what's going on myself. It's just that despite all the evidence I thought I had before I left, my instincts are telling me that Raphael di Lazaro isn't a drug dealer.'

'And the evidence for that interesting hypothesis is…?' The sarcasm in Lou's tone was blistering.

'Nothing yet. But I'm not coming back until I've proved it.'

'Or disproved it. In which case you may not be coming back at all. Alive, anyway.'

After she'd put the phone down, Eve wandered over to the dressing table. Her head ached from the effort of too much thinking, and from not wearing her glasses for two days, and her face was pale and drawn in the ghostly light.

She had never lied to Lou before, and never kept a secret from her—so why was she starting now? Lou only had her best interests at heart, so maybe it would have been a good idea to admit that Raphael hadn't exactly offered her a lift so much as deliberately used his stratospheric powers of seduction to get her into the car. Shortly after he'd offered her twenty thousand pounds to go home and shut up.

And while she was about it she might also have mentioned the bit about him stealing her phone, effectively cutting her off entirely from the outside world.

Why hadn't she said that?

Because, she admitted despairingly, all that added up to one thing. Against which her instinct wasn't worth a damn.

CHAPTER SEVEN

RAPHAEL woke up slowly, swimming groggily up through the fathomless depths of sleep inch by inch, so that he wasn't sure what was real and what he had dreamed.

Eve.

He heard the whisper of her voice in his ear, felt the caress of her breath on his neck, the cool pressure of her fingers on his skin. The scent of her filled his head, seeming to envelop him in warmth and comfort, until he opened his eyes expecting to find her beside him.

He was alone on the dark terrace. The candles had burned themselves out, and the coffee on the table was icy cold. But the subtle floral fragrance persisted. It took him a moment to realise it was coming from the soft wrap she had been wearing that evening, which was now spread over him.

Resisting the temptation to bury his face in it and breathe in her lingering perfume, he groaned quietly as the events of the evening slotted into place in his memory.

That kiss. The stupid, selfish, reckless pleasure of that kiss.

He'd intended to talk to her seriously when she came back, and make it perfectly clear that it had been a complete mistake. But like an idiot he must have fallen asleep. And she had come back and wrapped her shawl around him to stop him getting cold.

Not that there had been much chance of that, given the dream he'd been having...

The thoughtfulness of her gesture exasperated him as much as it touched him. Roughly he pulled the shawl off and stood up, stiffly stretching his cramped limbs, instinctively feeling in his pockets. Almost at the same moment that he remembered he still had her phone he realized it was missing and swore softly.

So the bit where she'd stood over him, her warm breasts rising and falling just centimetres from his face, while her hands moved over his body... That hadn't been a dream, then.

Making his way slowly upstairs, he yawned. At least a few hours' sleep would assuage the tiredness that numbed every muscle, every joint, every nerve in his entire body. If only it would be so easy to satisfy the deep ache of longing in his groin.

He paused outside the door to her room, torn apart by conflicting feelings he was too weary to analyse. But a second later all that was driven from his mind as a scream split the silence.

The man was so close behind her she could almost feel the heat of his breath on her neck. But it was always the same: the closer he got, the harder it was to keep running, until she felt as if she was wading through quicksand, and she knew that he would get her too, just as he'd got Ellie. She felt his hot hands grasping at her and let out a scream of pure terror.

'Shh... It's all right. Shh.... You're safe...'

A pair of strong arms seized her and she screamed again, writhing and clawing in terror.

'Eve! *Eve!* It's all right. It's just a dream. Shh...You're quite safe.'

It was Raphael's voice, close to her ear. It was his arms wrapped tightly around her, and his hands gentle on her sweat-soaked hair as they soothed away the nightmare. Overwhelmed with relief, she collapsed against his chest, desperately grateful for his warmth and strength.

Gradually her breathing steadied, and the trembling that racked her body grew less violent under the steady strokes of his hand. But she didn't want him to stop. The only sound in the still room came from the soft, rhythmic hissing sound of his hand against her hair and the steady thud of his heart beneath her ear. Sleep blurred the edges of her mind, drawing a veil of shadow over everything except his reassuring nearness.

Gently he laid her back on the pillows. She was dimly aware that her brief T-shirt had ridden up, but her embarrassment at the realisation was outweighed by the sudden desolation she felt at losing contact with his body. He pulled the covers back over her, then stood up.

Through half-closed eyes she watched him flex his tired shoulders, then bend to pick up her laptop and several scattered pages of notes for the article, which must have slid off her knee when she'd fallen asleep. As he reached over to turn out the light he paused for a moment and looked down at her. His face was lined with exhaustion, his expression guarded and remote.

'Thank you,' she murmured.

He shook his head wearily. Then switched the light off and was gone.

The sun was climbing higher into a sky the colour of delphiniums by the time Eve made her way hesitantly downstairs, stiff with shame and embarrassment at the prospect of seeing Raphael again.

So she'd managed to make an almighty fool of herself not once but twice in one evening. That was quite an achievement even by her standards.

And on both occasions Raphael had behaved with dignity and chivalry.

Damn him.

She'd woken early and tried to make some headway on the article, but no matter how hard she tried the words wouldn't come. Sienna and the retrospective seemed like light-years ago—part of another lifetime when she had known what she believed and had been charge of her own actions. Since then her heart seemed to have told her head its services were no longer required and staged something of a takeover, as last night's argument with Lou demonstrated.

She couldn't blame Lou for being worried. If she'd been a thousand miles away in England she probably would have been, too. It was just that here, in close proximity with Raphael di Lazaro, she had never felt safer in all her life.

She found Fiora in the salon, dusting the many photograph frames that crowded the surface of the grand piano. Golden motes danced in honeyed shafts of sunlight falling in through the three sets of French windows, suffusing the room with warmth.

'*Buongiorno, signorina.* You sleep good?'

Eve was just about to reply truthfully that, no, she'd had a dreadful night when she stopped herself. Judging from the meaningful look on Fiora's face, she would assume that meant one thing…

If only.

'Brilliantly, thank you, Fiora.' She beamed. 'It's so peaceful here.'

'*Si, signorina.* Signor di Lazaro, he always say that too. Here is the only place he sleep good.'

'Raphael?'

'Ne, Signor Antonio.' She sighed. 'He so tired *recentemente*. Now we know why…'

Tears filled her small dark eyes and, biting her lip, she reverently dabbed the duster over the photograph frame in her hand.

'Don't get upset, Fiora. I'm sure Signor Antonio will be out of hospital and back here where you can look after him in no time.'

'*Si, si…spero…*' Fiora sniffed, looking fondly down at the photograph. It showed a dinner-suited Antonio, arm in arm with someone who looked suspiciously like an Italian film star. 'Those *infermiera*—they not know him. He like things done just so. He not easy man. But underneath…he is good man.'

Not according to Raphael, thought Eve, who rather suspected that in his current state Antonio would neither know nor care how things were done. Out loud, she said, 'Have you worked for him for long?'

'*Trentacinque anni.* Thirty-five years. I start when he bring Isabella here as a young bride.'

'Raphael's mother?'

'*Si.*' Fiora replaced the photograph amongst the others. Most of them were of Antonio, formally dressed, with a variety of diamond-festooned beauties on his arm. Eve wondered which of them was Isabella.

'What was she like?'

Fiora reached over, picked up a small photograph from right at the back and handed it to her. It was of an astonishingly beautiful girl holding a little boy on her knee, and Eve's heart lurched as she recognised the child's huge dark eyes with their fringe of long lashes, his perfectly shaped mouth. Isabella was dressed to go out, wearing a simple dress of pale green silk-satin, with a tiny cluster of pink satin roses between her creamy breasts. She was looking straight into the camera, smiling radiantly, while Raphael, unsmiling, looked up into his mother's face with an intensity that made Eve's heart ache for him.

'Raphael is very like her.'

'*Si, l'aspetto,* perhaps. In personality he is like Signor Antonio.'

Eve looked up in surprise. 'Really? I thought—'

'Oh, they fight, *certo,* but is because they are just the same. *Ostinato, orgoglioso, difficile…*' She laughed. 'Always they think they are right! That is why they cannot get along.'

'She looks very beautiful. *Molto bella.* And very young.'

'*Ventuno* when they marry.'

Twenty-one. The same age as me, thought Eve in wonder. But found her gaze being drawn away from Isabella's luminous beauty back to the face of the little boy. Without thinking she stroked the pad of her thumb over his face, as if trying to soothe away the anguish that she saw in the dark pools of his eyes.

'You can see how much he loves her. Her death must have been devastating for him.'

She spoke out loud, but almost to herself, assuming that Fiora wouldn't understand. To her surprise, Fiora replied.

'*Si*. For a child to see such a thing…' Her voice trailed off and she shook her head sorrowfully.

In the short silence that followed, Eve's stomach gave a dramatic rumble.

'*Signorina, mia dispiace… Colazione! Poverino!* Come, come with me.'

Thoughtfully Eve replaced the photograph, this time positioning it right at the front, so it obscured Antonio and the filmstar. A thousand questions rose to the surface of her mind, like fish in a pool, but Fiora had already gone, hurrying off to the kitchen with an efficient rustling of skirts.

With a last glance into the sad eyes of the little boy, Eve followed.

Eve took her coffee out onto the terrace. In the shimmering morning light no evidence remained of what had taken place there last night, apart from a scattering of bruised rose petals on the flagstones beside Raphael's chair.

She bent to pick one up, crushing its soft flesh between her fingers and releasing its outrageously sensual fragrance. Instantly she was transported back to the moment when she had put her hand to his face and he had pulled her down to kiss him. A tide of bittersweet remembered ecstasy washed through her.

At that moment she'd been so sure of herself, so confident with her silly plan. Now it seemed nothing more than laughable. She'd thought that by getting closer to Raphael she would be able to see things more clearly, but, like Icarus flying towards the sun, she had been foolish and over-ambitious. The closer she got, the more he dazzled her.

Looking down, she saw that she was still holding the rose petal, but it was crushed and battered beyond recognition.

It seemed like an omen. She had been mad to think she could play games with a man like Raphael Di Lazaro and escape with her heart intact.

Beyond the terrace a broad sweep of lawn sloped downwards to a line of cypress trees in the distance, set along a stone wall. Suddenly the urge to get away from the house was overwhelming. Throwing down the tattered petal, she set off briskly in the direction of the trees.

As she got nearer she could see that the wall formed the back of a low, single-storey building with a sloping tiled roof. After hesitating, in case it was the home of one of the members of the villa's staff, Eve walked cautiously on. As she rounded the last corner she let out a gasp of pleasure.

Before her lay a swimming pool. A perfect, glittering oval of pure turquoise.

The building that she'd just walked around was built in the style of an ancient Roman bathhouse, with marble benches standing in the shade under the wide portico. Wistfully her gaze darted back to the water. The need to feel its soothing chill on her overheated skin was suddenly irresistible.

She opened one of the doors into the poolhouse and found herself in a stunning room decorated in pale, creamy tones. One wall was dominated by a huge mirror hanging over a marble topped counter on which an array of Lazaro cosmetics was arranged. Behind a screen of sandblasted glass in one corner there was a vast walk-in shower, and a pair of huge, squashy sofas covered in biscuit-coloured coarse linen stood either side of a low table on which piles of magazines were neatly stacked.

Feeling like Goldilocks in the Three Bears' house, Eve padded around, lifting the stoppers from jars and peering into cupboards.

She was hoping that someone would have conveniently left something for her to swim in, but, while the room contained every imaginable luxury, there was nothing so practical as a bikini.

Which left her with a choice. Bra and knickers, or nothing?

She didn't need to look at the verdigris clock set into the stone of the poolhouse wall to know it was almost lunchtime—the high, hot sun and her own gnawing hunger were evidence enough. But she felt better. There was something soothing about swimming, and length after length of rhythmic strokes had calmed her thoughts. It was a refreshed, restored and ravenous Eve who hauled herself reluctantly out of the pool.

In the end she had decided that skinny-dipping was a little too risqué; the thought of one of the servants—or, worse, Raphael—finding her, and standing over her as she got out of the water completely naked, had been enough to convince her that bra and knickers was the only option.

It wasn't a choice she had made lightly. The underwear she was wearing was a set Lou had made her buy on a last-minute shopping trip the day before she left, and had cost about as much as she would usually want to pay for a whole outfit. Including shoes and the bus fare home.

Although she'd been vociferous in her objections to the price, she secretly loved the semi-sheer organza bra and matching shorts. They were a delicate creamy cappuccino shade, and a butterfly nestled between the bra cups, its wings made of crisp lace in sugared almond pink. Swimming in things of extreme beauty had felt a little bit like wearing the crown jewels to dig the garden but, all things considered, it certainly beat the alternative.

And now she just had to get them dry again. She stretched out on one of the steamer chairs at the poolside and lifted her face to the sun, but realised within minutes that sitting in the heat for that long would be unbearable. She sat up, biting her lip. It seemed there was only one thing for it, after all.

She unfastened the bra and slipped it off, then wriggled quickly out of the damp shorts and draped them both over the chair at the side of the pool. Going back into the poolhouse, she picked up one of the glossy magazines from the pile on the table and began to flick through it. The next moment she gave an exclamation of delight as she came across a feature-length interview with Sienna.

It was a godsend—just the inspiration she needed to get her into the mood for returning to her own article. In fact, you could almost call it research. Throwing herself down onto one of the oversized sofas, Eve put on her glasses and began to read.

The surface of the water was smooth and still, and Raphael barely hesitated before plunging in with an impressively graceful dive. It felt delicious on his skin, and he swam a couple of lengths beneath its surface, grateful for the cool and quiet.

When he'd finally fallen into bed in the small hours he'd slept only fitfully, tormented by the memory of Eve's sweating, writhing body as he'd held her in his arms while the nightmare faded. A pale slice of blue sky had been visible through the gap in the curtains before sleep had come to him, and even then it had been plagued with more disturbing, sensual dreams that, on waking, had left him feeling raw and edgy with unfulfilled desire.

It was getting beyond a joke. For all his determination last night to make it clear to her that nothing more would happen between them, he could no longer pretend to himself that he wasn't seriously disturbed by her presence. It was an extremely unwelcome feeling, and one he was beginning to bitterly resent. Perhaps it was just as well he was going to Venice this afternoon.

Pushing through the water, he felt the life seep back into his heavy limbs. Yes, getting away from Eve for a couple of days would give him time to clear his head and maybe even run a few checks on her—find out exactly what sort of a threat she posed. In the meantime she'd be quite safe here with Fiora.

Considerably safer than she was with him.

The thought was an unsettling one. He swam faster, cutting through the water with long, savage strokes.

'Lazaro is my favourite label!' Sienna enthused in the interview. 'I love the fluid lines and feminine details. He has an amazing, instinctive understanding of women's bodies…'

Just like his son, thought Eve wistfully. She really ought to be getting back to her own article—her underwear would surely be dry by now. Reluctantly she replaced the magazine and, stretching indolently, padded out into the sunshine at the poolside.

She was just reaching for her things when a movement beneath the surface of the water caught her eye. Giving a tiny whimper of distress, she made a grab for her underwear, but in her haste the bra flew out of her shaking hands, making a graceful arc through the air before landing in the water.

Transfixed with horror, she watched it slowly float down towards the bottom of the pool.

Swimming under the water, Raphael saw something pale and gauzy drifting down from the surface. He glanced upwards through the turquoise depths and saw a figure, slender and golden as a sunflower, standing beside the pool. Her face was indistinct through the water, but there was no mistaking those long legs and generous curves. Grabbing the diaphanous piece of underwear, he kicked up to the surface and shook the water from his eyes as he placed it on the side.

Eve felt the blood rise to the surface of her skin as Raphael's gaze flickered dispassionately over her naked body. Frantically she looked around for something to cover herself up with.

Of course there was nothing.

Swallowing tears of utter mortification, she crossed her arms defensively over her breasts and wished she had the confidence to carry off the stark naked look successfully.

Failing that, a supermodel body would help.

'I was going to ask if this was yours, but actually I think I can work it out for myself.'

The lack of interest in his eyes was like a slap in the face after the passion of last night's kiss and the intimacy of waking up in his arms. Meeting his gaze as coolly as possible under the circumstances, Eve raised her chin a little.

'Top marks, Einstein. Now, if you've quite finished enjoying my humiliation, could I have it back, please?'

He sighed and lifted himself out of the pool in one lithe movement that made the muscles ripple beneath his glistening skin. Getting to his feet, he pushed the wet hair back from his forehead and came towards her, holding out the bra. In his masculine hand it looked absurdly girly and frivolous. And intimate—almost as if he wasn't touching an inanimate scrap of organza and lace but her own flesh...

Eve shrank back, despising herself for the shameful rush of sweet wetness that thought aroused in her.

'Are you going to come and get it, or do you want me to come over there and put it on for you?'

'No!' It came out as an embarrassing squeak.

'No, what?' he asked levelly. 'No, you're not going to come and get it? Or no, you don't want me to come and put it on for you? I hope it's the latter, because I have to admit my expertise lies more in the removal of these things.'

'Just give it to me,' she snapped. Darting forward, she shot out a hand and snatched the bra from where it swung, incriminatingly sexy, from his outstretched finger.

But, having got hold of it, she felt even more at a loss. What should she do now? If she were to turn and go back into the poolhouse she would give him a perfect view of her naked behind, and creeping backwards without turning round was just too ridiculously gauche and embarrassing to consider. Maybe she should just put her underwear on right here, in front of him? Another crimson tide of shame washed through her at the idea. Maybe not.

The realisation dawned that she was stuck there until he chose to leave. And he didn't seem to be in any hurry.

'I'm sorry. I had no idea you were down here.'

Miserably she faced him, aware that whichever way she crossed her arms there was no way she could cover her breasts up entirely. 'You don't have to apologise. It's your house.'

'Even so…' He stopped, seemingly struggling with what to say for a second. 'I wanted to apologise anyway. For what happened last night—'

'Look—please,' she interrupted desperately. 'There's really no need. I don't know what came over me. I don't usually—' She faltered, not wanting to put into words what had happened between them. Not wanting to be having this conversation. Particularly not wanting to be having this conversation while she was naked and clutching her underwear. 'Anyway,' she continued, looking down, 'it's over. Forgotten.'

From behind the damp tendrils of her hair she watched him nod and lift a hand to sweep the water from his face. 'I have to go away on business for a couple of days. I'm leaving this afternoon. Will you be all right here with Fiora?'

His casual words came out of the blue and hit her like darts, causing her head to jerk upwards with shock. And pain. Unexpected pain.

'Of course. I'm not a child. I don't need you to look after me.'

His eyebrows arched upwards sardonically. 'No?'

'No!'

'That wasn't how it felt last night.'

She heard the hiss of her own sharply indrawn breath. Humiliation instantly turned to rage, and blotted out everything else in its enveloping red mist. Planting her hands firmly on her hips, Eve lifted her head and glared at him with open hostility. *'That's not fair!* It was just some stupid dream… I didn't ask you to—'

She stopped, suddenly realising as he came towards her that in her anger she'd forgotten to cover herself, and was now standing in front of him with not a stitch on, hands on hips, in the manner of a cartoon stripper. All she needed was a pair of high heels and a string of fake pearls to complete the picture.

Brushing past her, he opened a door in the poolhouse and re-appeared a moment later with two towels. Draping one round his neck, he held the other one out to her.

But pride was a terrible thing. Naked, hurt, humiliated, at that moment Eve would have rather accepted help from Satan himself than Raphael di Lazaro. Sucking in her stomach, trying desperately to look as if her lack of clothes was a matter of supreme indifference to her, she pushed her shoulders back and eyed him coldly.

'You can tell Fiora that I won't be staying, so she's relieved of babysitting duty in your absence.'

There. That had wiped the mocking, self-satisfied smile off his face.

It also blew all her plans to tiny smithereens.

'Where are you planning to go?'

She shrugged. 'I'll find somewhere in Florence.'

Suddenly his face went very still. 'It's August. All the hotels will be full of tourists.'

Her chin shot up another inch. 'I'll just have to look at other options, then.'

Throwing him one last haughty glance, she turned round and sauntered slowly back into the poolhouse. It was maybe seven or eight paces, but it felt like miles. And every step was like walking on knives.

* * *

All the way back up to the house he cursed himself. He'd screwed up. Big-time. *He just couldn't stop himself from taking out on her the fact that she'd got under his skin, could he?* And now he'd blown it all.

The villa was cool and dim after the fierce midday glare outside, and it took a moment for his eyes to adjust. In the hallway he could hear Fiora's voice, the particular formal tone she adopted for the telephone. The next minute she came hurrying through to find him.

'Oh, Signor Raphael, *meno male*…!'

She looked stricken. Putting a reassuring hand on her shoulder, Raphael spoke calmly.

'What is it, Fiora? Is it the hospital?'

'Ne, signor. Polizia.'

Not a flicker of emotion showed on his face as he picked up the phone, but all the colour had drained from it.

'Marco? *Ciao.*'

'Ciao, Raphael. Look, I'll get straight to the point. It's not good news. Our chief witness in the case against Luca has met with a nasty accident.'

Raphael sucked in a breath, but his face remained stony as the detective elaborated on the girl's untimely end.

'There must be other witnesses?' Raphael pressed.

'Sure—but we can't exactly hold open interviews for every girl on the modeling scene. The fewer people who know about this the better. Especially if Luca's guys are going round picking off girls they're suspicious about.'

A chill spread down Raphael's spine as Eve's careless words came back to him *'I'm going to expose di Lazaro as a sleazy drug pusher…'*

'So, what now?' he asked the detective.

At the other end of the phone, Marco sighed. 'We watch him. It's all we can do until we find someone else who will testify against him—and keep our fingers crossed that it doesn't take too long.' Raphael could hear the frustration in his voice. 'He's getting more and more unpredictable. My feeling is that he's going to do something very stupid pretty soon. We just have to wait.'

Bloody, *bloody* hell.

Why had he taunted Eve like that? Now she was leaving—heading, in all probability, for Luca's flat—and it was entirely his fault. There was no way he could go to Venice now. He'd have to make his apologies to the award ceremony organizers and try to get Eve to stay at the villa, or get her on a flight back to London.

Unless he could persuade her to come with him to Venice…

'*Va bene,* Marco. Thanks for letting me know.'

As he replaced the receiver Eve appeared in the doorway. She had put on a long white shirt, but Raphael noticed with a painful clenching of his stomach that the fabric was too sheer to hide the swell of her bare breasts beneath it. In her hand she carried the wet bra.

She too must have been dazzled by the glare from outside, because she didn't notice him as she crossed the hallway. As he moved out of the shadow of the staircase she started violently, and let out a small scream of terror.

'You scared me!'

'Sorry.' He shook his head and laughed.

'It's not bloody funny!' she screamed. 'I know you think I'm completely stupid and naïve and *ridiculous*, but just give me an hour and I'll be out of your hair for ever. Then you can get back to your glamorous life and your clever, *sophisticated* friends, un-encumbered with such an embarrassing social liability! I didn't ask you to bring me here!'

Sobbing, she made a run for the stairs, but Raphael caught her before she reached them. For a moment she fought him off, but then found herself cradled in his arms, her cheek pressed against his bare chest while he rocked her and waited for the sobbing to subside.

As soon as she was calmer he disentangled himself as gently

as he could and stepped back. Another minute and no amount of railway timetables and international exchange rates would be able to contain the hard evidence of his desire.

'I'm sorry.' He gave her a bleak smile. 'And, before you say anything else, that's what I was laughing about. It occurred to me that I don't think I've ever apologised to anyone so much in my life before.' He sighed. 'Let's get one thing straight—I'm the one who's at fault here. Not you. And now I've got to go to Venice, so it looks like I won't have a chance to make it up to you…'

'It's fine,' she mumbled, clumsily scrubbing away the tears with the back of her hand. 'You don't owe me anything.'

'It's not fine.' He rubbed his hands over his eyes wearily, and Eve noticed there was a muscle twitching in his cheek. 'Look, why don't you come with me? I've got to go to the Press Photography Awards tonight, which will be extremely dull, but the dinner and champagne will make up for that a little. After that, I don't have to be back for a couple of days… I could show you round, maybe make you amend your appalling opinion of me. Have you ever been to Venice before?'

As she shook her head he could see conflicting emotions sweep across her face and he felt a flicker of optimism.

'Then it's simple—you have to come. We stay at the *palazzo* that belonged to my mother's family. It's pretty old and run down, but right in the centre of the city…' With heroic effort he softened his tone. 'Please… I'd like you to come.'

Slowly, mistrustfully, she looked up at him, as if searching to see whether he was joking or not. Her face was blotchy and red from crying, her lips swollen, but his heart gave a sudden lurch as she nodded.

'OK.'

Relief surged through him.

'Great. Go and pack. We need to leave in about an hour.'

Watching her run up the stairs, he felt the tension in the

knotted muscles of his shoulders and made an effort to relax. At least now he wouldn't have to worry about Luca getting his hands on her for the next couple of days.

He smiled ruefully to himself.

Which left him conveniently free to worry about keeping his own hands off her.

CHAPTER EIGHT

'YOU travel very light,' Raphael remarked drily, taking Eve's single tattered bag as they walked across the tarmac towards the Lazaro jet.

'I know. I'm sorry. I'm hopelessly scruffy,' Eve muttered, miserably aware of the pitiful figure she must cut in comparison with the designer-clad, high-maintenance women Raphael was used to.

Ever since they'd left the villa she'd been unable to meet his eye, frozen by sudden shyness in his presence. She'd accepted his invitation to go to Venice because, as she'd told Lou last night, she had no intention of returning to England without proof of his guilt or otherwise. But she was not yet so deluded that she couldn't see that it was also because leaving him now would be unbearable.

Walking beside him, she felt every cell of her body respond to his nearness. It was going to be an uncomfortable trip, she thought in anguish.

'I thought we made a deal? No more apologies—it's getting quite ridiculous. Anyway, you have nothing to be sorry about. You may not be at the cutting edge of fashion, but you certainly have style.' His tone was offhand—slightly bored, even—and he glanced down at her with a faint smile tinged with irony. 'Perhaps it's what your magazine would call "minimalist chic"?'

Eve looked down at her beloved but distinctly worn jewelled

sandals. 'I think it's what any magazine would call "in need of a makeover".'

'Well, I'm sure Nico will approve,' Raphael said, gesturing to the steward, who was coming towards them to relieve them of their small amount of luggage.

Last time Raphael had used Antonio's jet Catalina had been with him. Catalina and four cases, plus one large trunk containing all her cosmetics. A weekend away with her had always felt a little like embarking on an Edwardian Grand Tour.

'I haven't brought anything smart, I'm afraid. To be perfectly honest, I haven't actually *got* anything smart.'

'In that case we'll just have to go shopping.'

'No! I couldn't. I—'

Raphael cut through her objections. 'After you.'

Eve hesitated for a fraction of a second, then swallowed hard and went up the steps of the plane. In her head she repeated her usual pre-flight mantra. *Flying is statistically safer than crossing the road.* Adding hastily at the last minute, *Therefore I will not give Raphael di Lazaro the satisfaction of seeing me burst into tears on take-off.*

As he stood back to allow Eve to climb the steps to the plane ahead of him, Raphael found himself staring at her, drinking in her fresh simplicity. She was wearing yesterday's faded khaki combat trousers, rolled back to reveal slim, brown ankles, and had changed the damp shirt for a delicately embroidered and pin-tucked Victorian chemise with a low, lace-trimmed neckline that was simultaneously demure and sexy as hell.

Moodily he pushed a hand through his hair. Gone was the overt seductiveness of last night, but the shy self-effacement that had replaced it was having just as powerful an effect on his testosterone levels. Sticking to his resolution wasn't going to be easy, he realised grimly, barely managing a smile at the pilot who awaited them at the top of the steps.

'Welcome aboard, *signore, signorina.*'

'Thank you for getting everything ready for us at such short notice, Roberto,' Raphael said in his native tongue.

'*No problemo*, Signor Raphael. I am sorry to hear about the ill health of Signor di Lazaro…' Roberto drew Raphael slightly aside and said quietly, 'Signor Luca has requested the plane too, but I thought you and the *signorina* would prefer to fly alone. I hope that is all right?'

Raphael gave him a curt nod of acknowledgment, and the two men exchanged a swift glance of mutual understanding. Roberto had been instructed to monitor Luca's use of the jet very carefully indeed.

Eve was oblivious to this exchange, her fear temporarily forgotten as she took in her surroundings. She had expected a miniature plane, with rows of seats perhaps upholstered in a particularly plush fabric. In a daze, she found herself laughing at her own naïveté

This was laid out like a sitting room, with a sofa and armchairs at the front of the plane, facing each other around a low coffee table. Where the villa was decorated in perfect country-house style, the jet had obviously allowed Antonio the opportunity to play with contemporary design: the sofa was upholstered in scarlet leather, while the chairs were an assortment of suedes and velvets in various shades of charcoal and biscuit. The floor was covered in a thick cream faux fur rug, and one curved wall was painted with an enormous art-deco style mural depicting a whippet-thin woman reclining on a chaise-longue and sipping a cocktail through scarlet lips.

'I know,' Raphael said sardonically, coming to stand beside her. 'Hideous, isn't it? I think Luca had a hand in the design, which would explain why it looks like the waiting room in a brothel.'

Eve would have liked to ask him how he knew what a waiting room in a brothel looked like, but she was too shy. The flirtatiousness which had come so naturally last night, when she had still been under the illusion that it was all part of a calculated plan, had utterly deserted her today, leaving an awful stilted awkwardness in its wake.

'I'm not complaining,' she said taking the glass of prosecco he was holding out to her. 'It certainly compares quite favourably with the airborne cattle trucks that are my usual mode of transport.'

'Do you like flying?'

'Love it,' she said determinedly. Raphael thought she was immature enough already. There was absolutely no way she was about to admit to being as frightened as a rabbit on a motorway.

'Have you ever been on a private jet before?'

She attempted a mock-haughty look. 'Me? With my glamorous lifestyle? What do you think?'

He gave a sudden smile, which lit up his face and made her feel as if he had reached out and caressed her. 'I think no. It's completely against my principles, of course, but it's a great way to travel once in a while.' He held out his glass. 'Here's to the first time.'

She could feel the colour rush to her cheeks, just as the liquid heat was rushing into her pelvis. Glancing up in confusion, she met his gaze, and was unable to interpret the look in his hooded dark eyes. Was he testing her? Quickly she looked away.

'Here's to travelling in style,' she amended shakily.

'Or not,' he said, glancing disparagingly round at their opulent surroundings.

One thing that was no different on a luxury private jet from any less impressive aircraft, Eve discovered, was that the whole business of take-off was just as alarming. Try as she might as the plane began to accelerate along the runway, she could never quite get over the embarrassing, irrational fear that disaster was only seconds away, or shake off the suspicion that as the wheels left the tarmac it would probably be her last contact ever with solid ground.

Clutching her wine glass, she shut her eyes. The small plane sped forward, then plunged upwards into nothingness. There was a roaring in her ears as she felt the ground fall away beneath them, and the blackness behind her closed lids swirled and deepened.

The next thing she knew, Raphael was very gently prising her fingers off the glass. Taking it from her, he clasped her hands between his and kept them there, reassuring her with his quiet strength, until the plane had reached altitude and the fog of blind panic had cleared from her head.

Tentatively she opened her eyes, and found herself looking into his. For a second she saw there something dark and unreadable that sent shivers down her spine, but then the shutters came down again. He let go of her hands and leaned back on the scarlet leather upholstery with a look of amusement on his face.

'So take-off is one of the things you love most about flying, is it, Eve?'

She looked down into her lap and fiddled with a button on one of the many pockets of her trousers. 'I'm always worried it won't work.'

'I see,' he said gravely. 'You think that someone might have changed the laws of physics without telling you? Making it impossible under the new regulations for planes to stay up in the air?'

His voice was absolutely serious, but looking up at him from under lowered lids she saw the familiar mocking smile. The colour rose to her cheeks.

If she hadn't turned away she would have seen his face soften. 'Why didn't you tell me?'

'What? And shatter your image of me as a super-cool top international fashion journalist?' she muttered. 'It wouldn't have been fair to disillusion you.'

His lips twitched into a smile.

'Plus,' she went on, 'it's so stupid and embarrassing.'

'Don't be silly. It's neither stupid nor embarrassing—nor, in your case, particularly surprising.'

'Of course,' she said sulkily. 'It's completely predictable that I should be the kind of person who would cry on aeroplanes.'

'You didn't cry.'

'Not this time.'

'Anyway, that wasn't what I meant. I just meant that it's a basic human instinct to feel that the ground is a safe place and the sky isn't. And if there's anyone who lets themselves be governed by their instincts, it's you.'

She hesitated as the impact of his casual words sank in. Just a week ago, if anyone had said that to her, she would have protested hotly, arguing that she was governed by logic and intellect and good old-fashioned common sense. But she'd discovered things about herself in the last two days that had turned her world upside down.

And the strength of her instincts was one of them.

She looked up at him with troubled turquoise eyes. 'I just don't see how it can work.'

He sighed, pushing the hair back from his forehead. 'Think about it like this. It's all about forces. The plane's propellers create a thrust…'

He stood up and walked to the other end of the plane. It was only a small space, but he needed to put some distance between himself and her before every shred of reason or responsibility deserted him. There was no use in trying to kid himself that he was spouting A-level physics to reassure her, when he was all too aware it was just another tactic to divert his own mind from the much more interesting path it seemed hell-bent on taking.

'…which overcomes the drag of the air against the plane. The difference in air pressure on the upper and lower surfaces of the wing creates enough lift to support the weight of the plane in the sky. It all comes down to the friction between the opposing forces.'

She gave him a tiny, wicked smile. 'Ah, why didn't you say that at the start? Friction between opposing forces is something I understand perfectly. Thank you, Professor. Your mission has been successful.'

* * *

Below them the Appennine landscape looked calm and tranquil. Raphael wished he could say the same for his own emotions.

No, he corrected himself. *Not emotions. Hormones. Pheromones. Whatever else it was that made a man want to grab a woman and lose himself in her scent, her kisses, the pleasures of her body.*

Her perfume, the same one that had shrouded him in warmth last night while he had been sleeping, was tantalising him now, affecting his ability to think clearly.

And there was a lot he needed to think about. Since his conversation with Marco he'd been desperately trying to come up with some way of moving the investigation into Luca's drug dealing forward, and an idea had been growing at the back of his mind.

Deliberately he turned his face away from Eve, and with enormous self-control marshalled his thoughts.

Catalina was still living in Venice. She had returned to her home-town, where her parents still lived, after her break-up with Luca, to get over her drug addiction with their support and make a clean break from her old life. Raphael still had their number, and had made occasional contact with them over the past two years to enquire after Catalina's progress.

Maybe it was time to get in touch again.

He wasn't sure that Signora Di Souza would allow it, but if he could just meet up with Catalina maybe he could persuade her to give evidence against Luca and step into the breach left by the dead girl. But could he be sure he wouldn't be putting her in danger?

Raphael's relationship with Catalina had lasted just over two years, and, in spite of the fact that it had been Catalina who had walked out on him, he had always taken responsibility for the break-up himself. He had been too cold, too unwilling to commit. 'Emotionally frozen,' she had called him as she had hurled her bags into Luca's waiting car.

She was right, of course. No wonder she had fallen for the

laughing, charming Luca, whose extravagant romantic gestures were no doubt matched by effusive romantic words.

It must have been like travelling from Siberia to the Seychelles. But it had turned out to be a very poisoned paradise. Within six months Catalina had lost her contract with Lazaro as evidence of her drug habit became impossible to hide. She was lucky to have escaped Luca's clutches before she lost her life.

The rolling fields and verdant hillsides of Emilia Romagna were now giving way to the flatter land around the Venetian lagoon. Raphael glanced up at Eve to tell her that they were nearly there, but the words dried in his mouth. She had kicked off her sandals and was curled up in the corner of the sofa, her laptop balanced on her knee, her glasses perched on the end of her nose. In between bursts of typing she absent-mindedly twisted a lock of hair around one finger. She looked unbearably young.

His insides gave a painful twist of longing, and he had to clench his hands into fists just to stop himself from reaching out and stroking the delicately pale arch of her instep, which was just inches from his thigh on the scarlet leather.

At that moment she moved, putting the laptop to one side and stretching like a contented cat. Leaning over to the fruit bowl on the table, she picked out an apple, then, glancing up, saw him watching her and held it out to him.

'Do you want it?'

Her voice was husky from not speaking for a while, her expression artlessly, unconsciously inviting.

He gritted his teeth and forced a smile, hiding his discomfort behind a mask of irony.

'No, thanks. I may not be the kind of devout Catholic Fiora would like me to be, but even I know better than to accept an apple from a woman called Eve.'

Venice was a city for lovers, Eve thought wistfully, gazing out from the *vaporetto* at the couples walking over bridges and in and out of narrow alleyways, their arms wrapped around each other in sensual intimacy.

Since getting off the jet, Raphael had hardly spoken a word to her. His mind was clearly somewhere else. Or maybe it was just on some*one* else. He was probably remembering all the other times he'd visited Venice, with various glamorous, interesting women who wouldn't blush under the flirtatious banter of the *vaporetto* man, or jump so much they nearly fell into the canal when he took their hand to help them into the boat.

Out of the air-conditioned interior of the plane the air was as thick and sticky as warm honey, so it was a relief to feel the breeze in her hair as the boat moved through the water. At least she was here, she thought, in an attempt to be positive. She had wanted to visit Venice for as long as she could remember, though she had always imagined it would be with someone very significant.

Which, she realised with an agonising stab of despair, in a way it was.

Raphael dragged his gaze away from her and sighed inwardly. Venice was as grimy and glorious as ever, but he kept finding his eyes returning to Eve, enjoying her reaction to the sights more than the sights themselves. The emotions were so easy to read on her face—excitement, alarm, sadness, wistfulness—that he found himself constantly wondering what she was thinking.

And that was a dangerous path to go down.

She was probably eyeing up the local talent, he thought darkly. There were plenty of examples of Venice's beautiful youth to admire, and she was barely more than a teenager, *per l'amore di Dio*. That was what girls her age did.

He gritted his teeth and looked around, suddenly impatient to be off the boat and out of such close proximity with her. Tonight they would attend the awards ceremony, which would at least provide the relative safety of a crowd, and tomorrow he would make his excuses and go and meet Catalina. That done, they could return to Florence—hopefully with some good news for Marco.

'We get off here,' he said suddenly.

The *vaporetto* came to a rocky halt beside a small jetty. Bewildered, Eve followed Raphael, reluctantly taking the hand he held out to her as she stepped onto the wooden boards. He didn't meet her eye, dropping her hand again as soon as he decently could.

'Where are we going?' she asked, having to run a little to catch up with him as he walked off.

'Shopping.'

'Oh… What for?'

'I thought you said you had nothing to wear tonight?'

'Yes, but…'

She was almost running to keep up with him, and in the sultry afternoon heat it was unbearable. She lost her temper.

'Would you just please stop for a minute? I've had enough! We are *not* going shopping! For one thing I can't aff—'

'Here we are.' He stopped abruptly in front of a shop displaying the kind of clothes Eve had only seen on Hollywood's darlings on Oscars night. A stunning gown of midnight-blue taffeta studded with starry clusters of diamonds fell with effortless glamour from the flawless plastic shoulders of a disdainful-looking mannequin. The next thing Eve knew he had opened the door and swept her inside.

'Raphael,' she said, anger and embarrassment fighting within her. 'I said I—'

But the glamorous shop assistant was already beside them. Her face was almost as chillingly perfect as the model's in the window, but it broke into a seductive feline smile at the sight of Raphael.

'Signor di Lazaro, *bentornato*. It has been such a long time since we have seen you.'

'*Grazie*, Claudia. I know it's short notice, but I wonder if you can find something for my friend here, for tonight?'

'The photography awards? You are very naughty to leave it

so late, but I'm sure we can find something.' She turned to Eve, looking her over with dark, appraising eyes. 'This way, please.'

At the back of the shop Raphael deliberately turned his back on the row of changing cubicles and, sinking into one of the vast cream sofas, picked up a newspaper from the coffee table. Claudia understood her wealthy clients as perfectly as she understood fashion, and she had gone to considerable trouble to create an oasis where weary husbands would be only too happy to wait while their wives tried on clothes. The espresso machine was state-of-the-art, a plasma screen TV dominated one wall, and every imaginable publication—from the finance papers to tasteful top-shelf magazines—was represented in the pile of reading material.

It was an area designed exclusively for relaxation. So why did he feel as wound up as a racehorse under starter's orders?

In Columbia he'd found himself in situations that had been volatile and dangerous, but he'd never once felt at a loss as to how to react. He knew what he had to do, and he had no difficulty whatsoever in doing it, whatever the danger. How stupidly ironic that he should come home and find himself in a situation where he knew very well the right thing to do, but found himself ridiculously incapable of controlling his impulses to do the opposite.

In the changing cubicle Eve was still protesting, her soft, musical voice slightly breathless as Claudia ushered her out of her clothes. 'Raphael—listen. I can't afford to buy—'

'I'm not asking you to buy anything,' he said irritably. 'I'm dragging you to this event, so the least I can do is buy you something to wear.'

There was a little pause. When she spoke again her voice was slightly muffled, and he realised she must be taking her top off over her head.

'And what if I won't let you?'

He felt himself smile. 'You could always go in what you had on this morning.'

He heard her small gasp. The smile died on his face as lust kicked him in the ribs.

'*Bellisima, signorina.*' Claudia's voice reached him, the approval in her tone clearly audible. 'It looks beautiful on you. It certainly is a dress that makes a statement.'

'It's the statement it makes that worries me,' he heard Eve murmur. 'Something along the lines of Take me, I'm yours.'

Raphael thrust a hand through his hair. 'It sounds perfect,' he called out drily, trying to make light of the uncomfortable tension that was growing inside him. 'Am I going to be allowed to see it?'

'Uh-uh. No way. It's coming off right this second.'

Gritting his teeth against the vivid images *that* conjured up in his overwrought mind, he steeled himself not to turn round and stared stonily ahead.

But he hadn't noticed that the vast mirror in front of him reflected the row of changing cubicles. Beneath the door of the central one he could see a pair of smooth brown calves and slim ankles, and before his tortured gaze there was a slither of red as a dress slipped to the floor.

Hypnotised, he watched her step out of it on delicate feet.

It was the most perfectly erotic thing he'd ever seen.

He swallowed painfully, unable to tear his eyes away from the mirror. Each one of his senses was on hyper-alert, so that the rustle of silk as Eve slipped into another dress was almost unbearably tantalising, and the sound of the zip was like a physical caress. He found himself gazing helplessly at her small, highly-arched feet, watching her lift her toes, then rise up onto tiptoe for a moment before she stood still again.

There was a moment of silence, which was broken by Claudia's voice.

'Good. But you need to take your bra off to get the proper effect.'

Raphael shut his eyes and leaned his head back on the soft cream upholstery, crucified by desire. In his head he could picture the soft fullness of her breasts as she had stood by the pool that morning, naked, and furious as a kitten. Even when she was angry she had a fierce sweetness that just made him want to gather her up and kiss her quiet, as he had done in the street, when he'd seen her with Luca. He adored the way her clear turquoise eyes darkened almost to aquamarine, intensified by the prim librarian glasses she wore…

'*Signore?* Ready?'

Claudia stood back and held open the door.

The dress was made of gunmetal-grey silk, strapless and unadorned. As Raphael's eyes travelled slowly over Eve's body he felt as if the air was being slowly squeezed out of his lungs and replaced with lead. Her lovely feet had been encased into high-heeled grey satin shoes that made her long legs seem endless. Her hips swelled sensuously beneath the dull sheen of the silk, her slender waist was nipped in, and her glorious, voluptuous breasts spilled out of the top of the boned bodice in hour-glass perfection. Claudia had pinned up her hair and added a dark stain of lipstick to her mouth, giving it a sensuality that was almost indecent.

She looked beautiful. And sophisticated. And glamorous.

And he hated it.

Eve's heart was in her mouth as she stood in front of him. Maybe now he would take her seriously. Maybe now she would be the kind of woman who could seduce a man properly.

He stood up slowly and took a step towards her, his face as cold and hard as granite. Time seemed to stand still as his eyes moved over her and she waited for him to speak.

He said nothing. But then he didn't have to. His face said it all.

'You like it, *signore?*' asked Claudia nervously.

'It's fine,' he said tonelessly and, turning on his heel, strode off to wait at the cash desk.

White-faced and trembling, Eve fled back into the changing room.

CHAPTER NINE

As SHE walked out of the boutique Eve's glance was a blast of winter in the sweltering afternoon. Angrily she handed him the large, stiff-sided carrier containing the dress.

'As you insisted on buying the damn thing, you can carry it,' she said icily.

Without speaking Raphael took the bag and walked away. Eve had no choice but to follow.

The sky was the colour of a bruise as they made their way through *calles* and *campos* still busy with summer tourists and couples walking slowly, hand in hand. The melancholy beauty of the place added to Eve's utter despair as she hurried through the crowd in Raphael's wake. They seemed to be the only people who were rushing—everyone else moved at the leisurely pace of holidaymakers or with the languor of lovers. The anger that had pulsed through her in the shop as she'd torn the dress off and savagely scrubbed away every trace of the lipstick began to ebb away, but she tried desperately to hang onto it, knowing that underneath it there was nothing but a deep well of hurt and confusion.

They had reached a vast, wide-open square, surrounded by colonnaded buildings. As they made their way across it Eve suddenly realised why it seemed familiar. Familiar, and yet powerfully, breathtakingly unexpected in its scale and beauty. She stopped.

'Saint Mark's Square,' she breathed in awe.

Raphael turned round and saw her standing still, lost in wonder in the middle of the square. She was herself again: sweet, fresh-faced, all traces of the sophisticated beauty that had so unnerved him scrubbed away. His heart twisted painfully inside him.

'Something wrong?'

'No. I hadn't realised where we were, that's all.'

'Piazza San Marco. Home of the most expensive cappuccino in the world,' he said scornfully.

'It's amazing.'

'It certainly is. Amazing that tourists continue to fall for it.'

The sky had darkened slightly, lending a strange yellowish quality to the afternoon light. The heat was stifling now, and from out in the lagoon there was a distant rumble of thunder that made the crowds of people scattered around the square begin to disperse in search of shelter. Only Eve and Raphael did not move.

It was as if all the energy of the building storm was concentrated in the air that crackled between them. Eve's eyes flashed with fury.

'Of course I wouldn't expect *you* to find it in the slightest bit impressive or beautiful. You're completely above all that, aren't you, Raphael?

'Beauty?' he said softly. 'No. When it comes to real beauty I'm as much a fool as anyone else.' He took a step towards her, his face dangerously still apart from a muscle twitching in his jaw. 'What I can't stand is when it's cheapened and flaunted for the masses.'

She gave a little gasp as the viciousness of his words stung her.

'You *bastard*. You throw the Lazaro millions around like some sadistic fairy godmother, trying to turn me into Cinderella just so I won't show you up at this bloody ceremony, and then you complain when you don't like the results! Well, I'm afraid you just made a really bad investment. I'm *not* one of your glossy, glamorous, gorgeous women, and I never will be!'

The first fat drops of rain were beginning to fall from the livid sky. His face was pale in the unearthly light, but he gave a short, humourless laugh and dragged his hands through his hair.

'You just don't get it, do you? I don't *want* you to be one of my "glossy, glamorous women", for God's sake!'

She looked at him as if he'd just hit her, then with an agonised sob turned to run away. He grabbed her wrist and pulled her back, just as a monumental flash of lightning cracked the sky.

'You don't want me? Then stop playing games with me and leave me alone!' she screamed. 'If you don't want me, just bloody let me go!'

'No!' The word came from him in a jagged cry. 'I don't want you to be turned into one of those women because you're perfect the way you are! Eve, you're—'

But he didn't finish, because somehow his lips had found hers and he was kissing her as if his life depended on it. The warm rain mingled with the tears on her face, and she tasted of salt and earth and something pure and indefinable that was the essence of Eve, and he drank it in like a man who had been without water for days.

A crash of thunder echoed around the ancient walls of the square, and suddenly the rain was falling harder. Breaking off the kiss, he cupped her face in his hands and gazed at her in agony. Standing there in the pouring rain, with her thin chemise clinging wetly to her body, she was like an orphan of the storm. With a thick groan of anguish he realised that after she had tried on the dress she hadn't bothered to put her bra back on, and the glorious fullness of her breasts was as clearly visible through the transparent cotton as if she had been wearing nothing at all.

Suddenly he knew that he wanted her more than he'd ever wanted anything in his entire life.

She had heard the sound he made, and understood its meaning. Biting down on her swollen lip, she looked into his eyes and saw the torment he was suffering. Slowly, wonderingly, she reached up and, with a fingertip, swept aside the dripping lock of hair that was falling over his forehead, then brushed her lips against his in a gesture of acceptance and invitation.

His breathing was shallow and fast, his eyes almost black with the urgency of his need, and he gave another strangled groan. As a fork of lightning zig-zagged above them he took her hand and they began to run across the square, splashing through the puddles.

When they reached the other side Eve glanced back and gasped. 'The dress!'

The shiny crimson carrier bag was still standing where he had dropped it in the middle of the square.

'Leave it,' he growled, pulling her on.

He stopped at a huge wooden door. Dazed and disorientated with desire, Eve had no idea how they had got there, knew only that as Raphael pulled her up the steps and fitted a huge key into the lock she felt almost dizzy with the intensity of her craving for him.

They stumbled inside, her lips already seeking his before the door had even closed behind them. As it slammed shut they fell against it, mouths hungrily devouring what they had waited so long to taste. In the sudden quiet after the noise of the storm outside, Eve surrendered completely to the torrent of her own voracious longing. Spreading her arms out wide against the door, she arched her back in ecstatic submission, thrusting her breasts against the muscular wall of his chest, loving the exquisite agony as her peaked nipples rubbed against the layers of thin wet fabric that separated their flesh.

As their clothes began to dry a little on their heated bodies, another kind of wetness was flooding her from within. She ground her pelvis against him, feeling the unbearably enticing hardness of his arousal. Her fingers ached to reach for the belt of his trousers, but some sadistic instinct for prolonging the pleasure made her keep her hands pressed against the wall, until she felt she might scream with anticipation.

In the dim, underwater light of the hallway he tore his mouth from hers just as a spectacular flash of lightning illuminated his face. His expression was tortured, haunted, lost, and he pressed the heels of his hands into his eyes.

'Eve, I—'

She didn't wait to hear any more. While thunder shook the ancient casement windows some primitive animal instinct overtook her, making her reach out for him and grab the collar of his shirt. Pulling him roughly to her, she only had time to murmur three words before his mouth crashed down onto hers again.

'*I want you.*'

This time she was in control. She pushed herself away from the door and felt her legs part, her body curve towards his. His hands cupped her buttocks, caressing her, holding her against him, so that the throbbing of his desire merged with her own hot, pulsing need.

Blindly she felt for his belt, feeling the honeyed surge within her as her fingers found it and began to work on reaching their goal. Swiftly, deftly, she flicked the end of the belt out from its restraining loop, and was just about to undo it completely when his hand closed over hers.

'Not here.'

His voice was harsh and ragged. Placing a hand beneath each thigh, he scooped her up so that she was still facing him, straddling him, her eyes level with his. As he carried her effortlessly up the wide, sweeping staircase her gaze didn't flicker from his for an instant. And all the time her hands were very slowly undoing the buttons of his shirt. Freeing each one, she trailed a feather-light fingertip down his bare skin to the next, until they had reached the top of the stairs and only the button of his jeans remained.

His steps faltered as he felt her fingers work it open. Her turquoise eyes were hooded and opaque, and for a second her eyelids fluttered closed as her fingertips met the silken tip of his erection.

She felt the shudder ripple through his body, and he sucked in a shivering breath. Roughly applying his shoulder to the nearest door, he pushed it open, and in a couple of strides had crossed the room and laid her down on a bed.

There was something goddess-like in the way she rose up on her knees in front of him to finish what she had started. The storm continued to rage around them, but her face was perfectly composed, only the spreading darkness in her eyes and the swollen, rosy moistness of her parted lips betraying her hunger. With her eyes still fixed on his, her fingers moved downwards, and her lush mouth curved slowly into a sensual smile.

Button fly. The game could continue. Inch by devastating… ravishing…exquisite…inch, her caressing fingers moved down his throbbing hardness.

Clenching his fists against the unbearable pleasure, Raphael's groan was lost in an ear-splitting crash of thunder as he pushed her back onto the bed. Shrugging off his unbuttoned shirt, he closed his mouth over hers as his hands found the zip of her trousers and tugged them down over her knees, then turned their attention to her top.

The buttons were tiny. There were hundreds of them. And he didn't have her patience.

'Take it off!' he rasped.

She did as she was told, lifting her arms and wantonly wrenching the thin cotton top over her head in sudden desperation to be free of everything that restrained and separated them. As she did so Raphael drank in the sight of her slender body arching upwards, the delicate ridges of her ribs beneath the pale caramel of her skin, the gorgeous heaviness of her exceptional breasts. Unable to resist her any longer, he bent to brush his lips against one hard, thrusting nipple, then parted his lips to take the deep pink bud into his mouth.

A sharp shock of ecstasy quivered through her. She cried out—a high, keening sound of longing which echoed through the murky rooms of the silent *palazzo*.

Raphael raised his head to look into her eyes. In the purple storm-light his face was mask-like, inscrutable, the intensity of his response concentrated in his dark, glittering eyes. With swift, savage movements he stripped off the remainder of his own clothes and reached out to grasp her hips.

She was so wet. Almost deranged with the strength of his need for her, he ran his thumbs softly along her swollen, secret folds, marvelling at the liquid silkiness, loving her eager sweetness. He was hanging onto his self-control by the finest gossamer filament, and he knew that in a few more seconds he would be lost.

As he entered her he felt her tense suddenly. Looking into her eyes, he saw that her wanton confidence of a moment ago had gone, leaving a naked vulnerability that made the adrenalin surge within him.

'Eve,' he breathed. 'Oh, Eva...'

'Don't stop,' she sobbed. 'Please, Raphael—please, just keep—'

She gasped, unable to finish, as he gathered her into his arms and lifted her up. He positioned himself on the edge of the bed and she found herself sitting astride him, in exactly the same way as she had last night on the terrace. But this time she could feel him deep inside her, filling her in every possible sense.

With infinite tenderness he cradled her in his arms and began to rock her. Gently at first and then, as the shadows cleared from the deep pools of her eyes, she picked up the rhythm herself, added to it an urgency of her own. Instinctively she found herself putting her hands on his shoulders, moving to take some of her weight onto her knees, giving her more freedom to tilt her pelvis towards him, taking him deeper and deeper into her with each blissful thrust.

Their eyes met and locked. His were filled with an emotion that she couldn't read but wanted desperately to understand. She let herself fall into their dark, troubled depths and he wrenched his gaze from hers, buried his face in her neck, breathing her in, tasting the delicious dampness of her flesh. The sensation of his lips on the sensitised skin of her shoulder and the taut column of her throat seemed to travel like quicksilver straight down into the molten core of her, adding a spark to the smouldering heat between her thighs.

Just when he thought he could hold off the moment of sweet release no longer, he felt her stiffen and grow still in his arms, then cry out in joy and surprise.

The pleasure he got from hearing that sound was inde-scribable. Even his own blissful, earth-shattering climax a second later couldn't beat it.

In the aftermath of the storm the air was cooler. As the sweat dried on their exhausted bodies Raphael felt Eve shiver, so without letting her go he tugged back the layers of crisp sheets and slid between them.

They lay in silence, their limbs entangled, his head resting lightly against the silken pillow of her breasts while one hand softly caressed the hollow of her waist. The sense of deep peace that had overtaken him as their lovemaking had reached its climax was already beginning to ebb away as the implications of what had happened hit home.

He'd written her off as an unscrupulous journalist, out to do a kiss-and-tell exposé. He'd kept her with him because he didn't trust her. *Because he was supposed to be protecting her.*

And now he knew that her innocence was for real. And he had failed her. He was supposed to be protecting her, but he'd been so carried away by his own lust that he hadn't even managed to use a condom.

A tide of guilt and self-loathing swept through him.

'You should have told me.'

His voice was just harsh whisper, and her hand, which had been running through his hair, suddenly stopped its rhythmic stroking.

'Told you what?'

'That you were a virgin.'

'Would it have made any difference?'

He sighed heavily. 'Of course. Of course it would.'

His words cut into her like sharpened blades, until the ornate plaster cornicing she had been staring at on the ceiling above the bed disappeared in a blur of tears.

That was what she had been afraid of. To him what had just taken place between them was obviously just a casual encounter. Had he known she was a virgin he would have felt under too much pressure to make it into something more. She blinked hard. It was bad enough that he had found out she was pathetically inexperienced without her burdening him with childish emotional outbursts as well.

'I didn't tell you because it isn't important.'

'I would have been more…gentle. And gentlemanly. I'm sorry.'

'I thought you said no more apologies?' She gave a laugh that sounded almost like a sob. 'Or were you fishing for compliments? You were perfect. It was…' She hesitated, lost for words, unconsciously caressing him again as they were both overwhelmed by remembered sensation.

Languidly she ran her fingers through the silky length of his hair, watching it fall back onto her skin, starkly black against the creamy white of her breasts. Every now and again she caught a glimpse of silver glinting in the dark mass. This tiny, unexpected sign of vulnerability touched her unbearably.

'You're going grey,' she said softly, singling out one pure silvery strand.

Sitting up, he gave a bleak laugh. 'Of course I am. I'm old. Too old for you.'

'Says who?' Behind him her voice was achingly tender. 'Your mother was the same age as me when she married your father, and he was a lot older than her. Fiora told me.'

She felt him stiffen. 'Come on,' he said abruptly throwing back the sheets. 'We have a ceremony to attend.'

'Well, I hope the designer gene has been passed down. Because since we left the dress in Saint Mark's Square, all I have to wear is this sheet.'

Buttoning up his jeans, trying not to think about the delicious circumstances of their unbuttoning, he looked at her and was caught off guard for a moment by her astonishing beauty. Her golden hair was tousled, her skin a warm honeyed apricot against the white of the sheets, and her aquamarine eyes shimmered with the afterglow of passion, and what looked like tears.

'I don't doubt you'd carry it off beautifully,' he commented sardonically, walking towards the long wall of built-in cupboards. 'But fortunately you shouldn't have to.' Throwing open one pair of doors, he revealed a row of dresses in a kaleidoscope of colours.

From the bed, Eve gasped.

'Whose are they?'

'My mother's. I don't think she'll be needing any of them tonight, though,' he added with a twisted smile.

While Raphael went back downstairs to find their luggage Eve wound the sheet around herself and moved over to the wardrobe. The luxurious fabric of the countless dresses caressed her fingers, and the faint, unmistakable fragrance of gardenia drifted up from their silky folds. An image of the beautiful, laughing woman in the photograph came back to her, and she felt the sting of tears behind her eyes again. How could Raphael bear to look in here?

She started as he came back with the bags.

'Have you found anything?'

'No. I mean—yes. But there's so much… I wouldn't know where to begin.'

Her heart ached for him as he began to rifle through the rails. Not a flicker of emotion showed on his face.

'Nothing black or red. Or grey. I don't want you looking sophisticated. I'd much rather you looked like yourself.'

He pulled out a selection of dresses in beautiful shades of

dusky pink, duck-egg blue, pistachio-green and ivory, and threw them down onto the bed.

'Try these to start with.'

'They're gorgeous.' She picked up the pink one from the top of the pile, touching its lacy hem with awe. Behind her, Raphael was busy unzipping his battered leather flight bag and shaking out his dinner jacket, so she took advantage of his preoccupation to drop the sheet and slip into the dress.

'There are probably shoes in there somewhere as well,' he said, without turning round.

With the dress still unfastened at the back, she bent to look in the bottom of the cupboard. Sure enough there were rows of shoes arranged neatly on racks—some of them in boxes, some in soft drawstring bags, some just swathed in tissues.

'How come everything's still here, just as she left it, after all this time?' she asked, taking out a perfect pair of fifties-style slingbacks in palest pink satin.

Raphael shrugged. 'My father didn't want to get rid of them. I guess it was easier to store them here than move them.'

'He must have loved her very much.'

'Not at all. It was the dresses he loved. Most of them are his own designs.'

The bitterness in his voice made her wince. 'Oh, Raphael, no! Surely that's not true? He must have loved her!'

Raphael had put the large, square black case he had brought with him from Florence on the bed, and now he snapped it open. Eve couldn't see what it contained, but it looked sinister-like a gun case. She realised she didn't feel remotely concerned.

I trust him with my life, she thought matter-of-factly. *It doesn't make sense, but I can't help it.*

'He never showed any signs of it. I don't think he ever stopped trying to change her into something she wasn't.'

'What was she like?'

'Sweet. Funny.' His fingers faltered for a second as he realised

who else that description fitted, but he didn't stop what he was
doing or look up. 'She couldn't help but laugh at the absurdities
of the fashion world, which my father always says drove him
mad. To him, fashion is an extremely serious matter.'

'Why did he marry her, then?' Eve asked as, holding the pink
dress up at the front, she slipped her feet into the slingbacks.
Reaching backwards to slip the straps over her heels, she heard
the mechanical whirr of a camera shutter. So that was what the
case contained. Startled, she looked up—straight into the lens.

'Wh-what are you—?'

'When I see something beautiful I want to photograph it.' His
eyes were narrow and unsmiling as he looked at her, then he
raised the camera again and continued. 'She was the daughter of
a *duce*—Italian aristocracy—and she was very lovely. She was
his *muse*—' he said the word scornfully '—before she was his
wife.'

He was lying on the bed, propped up against the pillows, his
face obscured by the bulk of the camera. Breaking off for a
moment, to adjust something on the long zoom lens, he glanced
up at her suddenly. 'Put the blue one on now.'

She did as she was told, stepping quickly out of the pink dress,
still in the delicate satin shoes. The camera whirred on.

'Go on,' she prompted gently.

'From the start she was a target for the paparazzi. Beautiful
young heiress married to celebrated designer—paparazzi
heaven. But she hated it. She was young, shy, insecure—completely unsuited to the role he thrust her into.'

Totally absorbed in what he was saying, Eve slipped her arms
into the blue dress. Without attempting to fasten it, she turned
to look in the mirror, giving Raphael a perfect view of her bare
brown back. He fired off a quick succession of shots, hoping to
capture the way the late-afternoon light was casting a soft halo
around her hair and turning her skin to gold.

She looked at him over her shoulder as she took the dress off again, picked up the green one from the pile and unzipped it. 'So what happened?'

'He couldn't see how much she hated it. Publicity is everything to him. He couldn't see how bloody awful it was for her—how hounded she felt. It got steadily worse after I was born, because she tried even harder to avoid it then—for my sake—which just made her an even more tempting target. Then one day she took me to the dentist. As we came out there were a couple of paparazzi who started hassling her, calling out, taunting her to get a shot. It really got to her. She stepped out into the road to get away from them.'

Eve was aware of the absolute stillness in the room and found herself hardly daring to breathe, the pale green dress draped loosely around her. Fiora's words came back to her. *A terrible thing for a child to see...*

'The car had no chance of avoiding her. Afterwards the driver blamed himself, but it wasn't his fault.'

All that was audible in the sudden silence was the rustle of silk as she crossed the room and slipped onto the bed beside him. She spoke quietly, firmly, but with incredible gentleness, taking his frozen hands within her own and holding them tightly.

'No, it wasn't his fault. Or your fault. And it wasn't your father's either.'

Crucified by the pain of things he had never spoken of to anyone before, Raphael pulled away and strode over to the window.

'It was. He should have...'

He faltered, then cleared his throat before continuing in a low, even tone. 'He should have done more to protect her. From all of that. If he had loved her he would have protected her.'

For a long moment neither of them moved. Then, straightening abruptly, he turned back to where Eve sat in the rumpled wreckage of the bed.

'Anyway—enough of all that. We're going to be late.'

Savagely doing up the buttons on his shirt, he realised she'd done it again. Drawn things out of him that he hadn't even wanted to admit to himself. If it was a journalistic tactic she was bloody well wasted on that silly celebrity gossip rag. She ought to be on the political desk of a top broadsheet.

'Could you do the zip for me?'

She stood beside him, offering him her bare brown back. The bones of her spine were like a tapering string of pearls beneath her gleaming skin, but infinitely more delicate and precious. Feeling the breath catch in his throat, he swept her hair aside and, with massive self-control, averted his gaze from the secret, sensual hollow at the nape of her neck. After tugging the zip upwards, he stepped away.

She turned to face him, and he noticed how the dress—*that* dress—brought out the green of her eyes, how they shone with compassion and understanding.

'Do I look all right?'

For a moment he didn't trust himself to speak—which, he reflected bleakly, was somewhat ironic.

She was supposed to be the one he didn't trust.

CHAPTER TEN

THE world looked completely different as they emerged from the *palazzo* after the storm.

The city's crumbling, softly coloured buildings were blotchy from the deluge, but the sky had shaken off its heavy purple clouds and was now a clear, sparkling blue. The evening light falling on the rain-soaked streets turned them into an enchanted city of pearl and gold.

But it wasn't just Venice that had changed, Eve acknowledged, shivering slightly in the warm evening. She had too.

Raphael's lovemaking had transformed her—invisibly, indefinably, irreversibly. It was as if someone had whispered to her the secrets of the universe, or taken her hand and given her a glimpse of paradise.

Walking along the narrow *fondamenta* beside her, Raphael seemed tall and distant, and though she desperately yearned to touch him she didn't dare breach the small distance between them. Since his revelations about his mother's death he'd been withdrawn to the point of distraction. Only when she'd finally finished getting ready and had stood in front of him had his face shown any flicker of emotion.

And then she'd realised that she was wearing the pistachio-green dress his mother had on in that picture.

She had stammered horrified apologies, but he had laid a finger on her lips to silence her.

'No apologies—remember? It's fine.' But his voice had been oddly flat.

Now, as he stood to one side to let her cross a narrow bridge, she stole a surreptitious glance up at him. No wonder she was completely incapable of taking adequate notice of her incredible surroundings. Even Venice paled into significance compared with his exceptional good looks.

He was born to wear evening dress—his dark, brooding beauty was set off to perfection by the impeccably cut black suit, his long dark hair for once slicked back from his face, showing off its aristocratic hauteur. He had never looked more gorgeous, or more out of reach.

They reached the other side of the bridge and he suddenly looked down at her, his face softening slightly.

'Nearly there. I'm not being a very good tour guide, am I? I keep forgetting you haven't been here before. I should be pointing out all the sights.'

She shook her head, looking down at the pale pink satin shoes so that he wouldn't see her blush as she lied blatantly, 'That's OK. I'm just drinking in its incredible beauty. I don't need to know any more than that.'

'Oh, I don't know,' he said softly. 'To really fall in love with the place you need to get to know it, not just admire what it looks like from the outside.'

'Yes, well, maybe you're right. But perhaps I don't want to get to know it.' Eve looked up at him with a painful smile. 'If I fall in love with it I'll never want to leave.'

Eve hadn't been sure what to expect the awards ceremony to be like, but she had been prepared for a similar media circus to the perfume launch.

She couldn't have been more wrong. The event was being

held in one of the old *settoecento palazzos* just off the Grand Canal, but whereas the watchword at the perfume launch had been glitz, here it was restraint. No red carpet covered the narrow stone *fondamenta* at the top of the steps from the water, and the only cameras in the immediate area were held by curious tourists, delighted at the spectacle of such smartly dressed partygoers.

They entered a vast reception hall filled with chattering women in rainbow-coloured silks and chiffons, and distinguished-looking dinner-suited men. Letting go of her arm, Raphael turned to her and murmured, 'Wait here,' before disappearing into the crowd.

Without the silent strength of his presence Eve felt suddenly bereft. She sighed, looking up at the high, vaulted ceiling. It was a feeling she was going to have to get used to. In a couple of days they would return to Florence, and then she would go back to England.

Alone.

Some time this afternoon, somewhere in the bliss of Raphael's arms and the paradise of his bed, she'd reached the point of no return.

She had fallen hopelessly in love with him.

Literally.

Finding out that he had been involved in Ellie's death would be intolerably agonising now. She just couldn't risk it. The only thing to do was leave while her illusions and her memories were intact.

Of course, she thought, with a momentary flash of desperate hope, there was always the chance that she would discover something that categorically ruled out Raphael's involvement in Ellie's death, and then…

She gasped as someone slipped behind her, covering her eyes with a big, strong hand.

'Guess who?'

'I…I don't…'

'Come on, *bambino*, surely you haven't forgotten me already? I am destroyed.'

The hand was removed, and she turned round.

'Luca! What on earth are you doing here?'

'Now I ask myself the same question,' he said tragically. 'I come all this way to rescue you from the extreme dullness of my big, grown-up brother, and you not even recognise me. My life is ended...'

'Don't be so silly,' she laughed, hitting him playfully on the arm. 'It's lovely to see you again.'

'And you, *cara*... And you.' A big smile spread across his face. 'You look *sensazionale*,' he said warmly, walking around her. 'Delicious, in fact. I could eat you with a spoon.'

'Stop it,' Eve retorted, but she was smiling. There was something very charming about Luca's flirting, especially after Raphael's distance since they had arrived at the ceremony.

'I called you,' Luca said reproachfully. 'I was going to take you out to lunch and give you all the gossip from the retrospective party for your article. But—' he raised his hands in a gesture of helplessness '—you don't answer my calls.'

'Calls? I didn't—' She broke off abruptly. That must have been when Raphael had taken her phone.

Suddenly an idea occurred to her. The smile faded and a worried frown creased her forehead. 'Luca? Could I ask you something?'

'Of course, *bella*, and I can absolutely guarantee that the answer will be yes.'

'No, I mean it. Something serious. About Raphael.'

He sighed theatrically and rolled his eyes. 'If you must. I, however, am much more interesting. Are you quite sure there's nothing you'd like to ask about me? Like which hotel I am staying at? The room number, perhaps?'

But she was not to be diverted. There might not be any love between the two brothers, but Luca must know Raphael better than most. He more than anyone would know of any involvement with drugs in Raphael's past, and because of the animosity between them would no doubt be only too pleased to share the information.

She hesitated, unsure how to phrase the many questions that were crowding into her mind.

Luca had bent a little, and was looking questioningly, speculatively, into her face. His eyes were dark, and seemed to glitter with something slightly malevolent. She shook her head and looked away, confused.

'*Cara?*' Luca prompted.

The moment had passed, and with it her opportunity to find out that her suspicions were correct, or to lay her worst fears to rest once and for all. It was like some sadistic gambling game, with her future happiness as the stakes.

'Doesn't matter,' she muttered in anguish.

Through the crowd she could see Raphael coming back towards her, two glasses of champagne in his hands. There was something hypnotically charismatic about him. Eve found it impossible to tear her eyes away from him, and she experienced an exquisite flashback to the events of the afternoon. Breathlessly she relived the feeling of his mouth on hers, the naked longing on his face as he'd carried her up the stairs.

She felt her stomach flip as he looked up and met her eye, and she had the most delicious sensation that he was remembering exactly the same thing. But the next moment his expression had changed to one of open hostility.

'*Che diavolo…?*'

'Now, now, big brother. Watch your language. We are not in the backstreets of Columbia now.'

'Why the hell are *you* here?'

'Funnily enough I nearly wasn't, as the Lazaro jet that was supposed to be bringing me was suddenly unavailable.' Luca's tone was light, and his smile didn't fade, but there was no mistaking the malice behind his words. 'You obviously don't take enough interest in the Lazaro business, Raphael. If you did, you'd know that we are one of the major sponsors of these awards.'

Raphael glanced around, wondering if any of the smartly dressed guests were actually Marco's men undercover. He hoped so.

'I'm surprised,' he said sardonically. 'It's unlike Lazaro to be involved in anything so worthwhile.'

'Not my idea of good PR, I have to confess. You're absolutely right—usually we prefer to go for sponsorship of slightly more—' Luca glanced around disdainfully '—fashionable events. Alessandra Ferretti always did have a soft spot for you, though, big brother. She obviously managed to twist Father's arm.'

'How is he?' Eve interrupted, noticing the murderous hatred in Raphael's eyes.

Luca shrugged. 'He has not woken up yet.' He rolled his eyes. 'Though why he is so tired I have no idea. I am the one who does all the work.'

'It's the sedation,' Raphael snarled through gritted teeth. 'I spoke to the hospital a little while ago. They're keeping him sedated.'

'Hadn't we better find our table, Raphael?' Eve asked, gently touching his arm and willing him to look at her. Anything to break the terrifying tension that froze the air between the two men.

'Of course.' Luca was suddenly the picture of solicitousness. 'You must go—we can finish our conversation later, *mia cara*. You had something you wanted to ask me, remember?'

Eve felt Raphael tense at the endearment, and, hooking her arm through his, pulled him away from Luca.

'No, no—forget it. It really doesn't make any difference now.'

Eve's initial disappointment that she wasn't sitting next to Raphael at dinner gave way to relief as the man who was to be seated on her right introduced himself. Paul was young, enthusiastic, and, much to her delight, from London. Suddenly the evening didn't look as if it would be such a struggle, and her worries about letting Raphael down with her poor Italian, her sketchy knowledge of photography and her ignorance of the grim realities of global conflict evaporated, as they immediately started swapping notes about their favourite places. Once they'd established a shared passion for a particular deli in Notting Hill there was no stopping them.

However, it didn't stop her from feeling a breathtaking pang of jealousy when the seat next to Raphael was taken by the *über*-sexy Alessandra Ferretti. Dressed in a clinging, tan-enhancing dress of flame orange, she had obviously waited until everyone else was seated before coming to the table to ensure maximum attention. Eve had to admire her faultless instinct for a PR opportunity.

Everyone else seemed to be admiring her cleavage in the low-cut dress.

Immediately Alessandra drew her chair closer to Raphael's and began talking to him. Eve was too far away to hear any of their conversation, but although she wasn't great at understanding Italian, she was a lot better at interpreting body language.

Alessandra's was saying *private party* in loud, clear tones.

'Have you tried their buffalo milk mozzarella?' Paul asked, as waiters brought out plates of antipasti. 'They get them flown in every Thursday from a little producer in Southern Italy.'

Eve shook her head, trying to concentrate on what he was saying, but his passion for this particular Italian cheese faded into the background as she studied Alessandra's greater passion for a particular Italian photographer. Her movements were so confident and lazily seductive as she leaned back in her chair, sipping wine and laughing, or tossing back her long mane of dark hair, that to a casual observer she looked completely at ease. But Eve had noticed the intense, rapacious look on her face in the candlelight as she spoke to Raphael and Raphael only.

He seemed a million light-years away, the events of the afternoon as insubstantial as the mist that was falling over the darkening canal outside. But then suddenly he looked up and gave her the ghost of an ironic smile, and she felt better.

Once the main course had been cleared away the main purpose of the evening could get underway. A distinguished-looking man in his sixties took the podium at the front of the room, and silence fell as the lights were dimmed and he began to speak. Eve couldn't catch much of what he was saying, but was content to sit back in her chair, sleepy and replete, and let it all wash over her.

A huge screen behind the podium had been displaying a constant slide show of images, but now the compère stood aside as the photographs competing for awards in each category were shown. One by one the winners wove their way through the tables to collect their awards. Eve's hands grew tired of clapping as the evening wore on, and the pictures all blurred together as her mind produced images of its own in glorious Technicolor. The wet tendrils of hair dripping down Raphael's sun-tanned neck as he'd wrestled to open the door of the *palazzo*. The ravaged, tortured look on his face as she had pulled him towards her in the dark hallway. His hands, brown against the pale skin of her hips, as he had raised them up to enter her...

She bit back the soft moan of desire that threatened to escape her and looked over at those hands now. Strong, artistic and long-fingered, they were playing idly with a knife, but the rest of him was completely still, his expression absolutely blank. Gradually emerging from her fantasy world, and inching back into the present, Eve noticed that all eyes around the table and in the rest of the room were upon him—and suddenly there was a deafening explosion of applause.

'Bloody talented bloke,' said Paul admiringly, clapping furiously.

Raphael rose from his seat and walked towards the podium and the huge image on the screen behind it. Eve gasped as she took it in. Even without her glasses, its power was undeniable.

It showed a woman holding a chubby, laughing baby. Immediately the viewer's eye was drawn to the child's face, with its clear blue long-lashed eyes and dimpled rosy cheeks. It was a universal image of innocence and sweetness, and only after seeing all that did one take in the rest of the scene. The mother was barely more than a child herself—thin, hollow-cheeked, dead-eyed. The arms that held the baby were skin and bone, the blackened veins clearly visible beneath her papery skin. On the grimy bed beside them lay a child's teddy bear—and a used syringe.

Raphael reached the front, where Luca waited to present him with his award. There was an awful moment when Luca held out his hand and Raphael hesitated, his face darker than the storm-clouds that had gathered over the city that afternoon.

Ignoring Luca's outstretched hand, he turned to the clapping audience. The room fell silent as he began to speak.

'I am honoured to accept the award for Photographer of the Year and, as is only appropriate, will be sharing the prize money between a couple of charities—the Orphans of Heroin in Columbia, and the Drug Recovery and Rehabilitation Centre we set up in Florence two and a half years ago.'

There was a burst of applause, which he swiftly quelled. 'I'm humbly aware that it is the subjects of my pictures who are exceptional, not the person taking them. I'm hugely grateful to anyone who trusts me enough to photograph them...' His eyes flickered over Eve, sending an explosion of sparks through her central nervous system. 'But I hope that, in time, the people of Columbia may have cause to be grateful to me too. For exposing their situation to the world, and continuing to work towards improving it.' He paused, and the silence in the room was almost tangible. 'The work will continue until the menace of drugs and those who produce and profit from them is removed.'

Only as his words were drowned out in another sea of applause and the scraping of chairs as everyone stood up did Raphael turn to face Luca and shake his hand. It looked more like the sealing of a solemn vow than a salutation of thanks or congratulation.

Alessandra Ferretti wasted no time in offering her congratulations as Raphael came back to the table. Wrapping herself around him, she kissed him lingeringly on both cheeks, then drew him swiftly aside before Eve had a chance to even leave her place.

'I've organised a few publicity shots for all the major glossies that should bring in lots of cash for the charity,' she was saying as she led him away.

He turned and met Eve's eye, holding it for the briefest moment before he was swallowed up by the crowd.

'He's a genius. A bloody genius.' Paul sighed wistfully as they stood in front of Raphael's photographs in the gallery.

He had brought Eve up to the *palazzo*'s long gallery, where all the photographs of the nominees were on display. She had dutifully admired the two he had entered—of angular bluish landscapes which, he informed her, were soon-to-be-melted polar ice caps—but found herself drifting on a cloud of cautious euphoria to Raphael's work.

'Look at the composition there,' Paul was saying enviously, pointing to a shot of some little boys with grubby faces, playing football in a dusty road. The arid monochrome of the road contrasted vividly with the lush fields that surrounded them on both sides. Eve peered more closely, wishing she hadn't been too vain to wear her glasses.

'The emotion in some of these shots is just incredible,' Paul continued. 'These people were regarded as villains, the scum who produce the stuff our A-listers are busily shoving up their nostrils, but Di Lazaro's given us the chance to see them differently. Given them—I don't know—a sort of…'

'Dignity,' Eve finished for him. She found that a film of tears had blurred the grimy, smiling faces of the little boys.

'Ah, there you are, Eve.' Alessandra Ferretti appeared from nowhere, on a cloud of extremely heavy perfume. 'Raphael was asking for you. He's going to take you home now.'

She spoke as if Eve was some overtired child who was spoiling the party for all the grown-ups. Determinedly Eve kept her gaze fixed on the children enjoying their game of football on a dusty road in Columbia. She was trying to imagine Raphael there, just a few feet away from them. Like the baby in the winning picture, two of the boys were smiling straight into the camera, and Eve wondered what Raphael had been saying to them.

'He's waiting.'

There was a sharp edge to Alessandra's voice, but it couldn't burst the bubble of joy inside her.

She said an affectionate goodbye to Paul and followed Alessandra along the gallery. 'Tell me about the charities Raphael mentioned. The Orphans of Heroin in Columbia and—what was the other one? In Florence?'

'The Drugs Recovery and Rehabilitation Service. He set that one up as a helpline initially. In our industry—' she said patronisingly, as though she and Raphael shared a glamorous existence that would be entirely alien to the likes of Eve '—we see lots of people go down that route. Drugs are an inevitable part of the fashion scene. But he wanted to provide a point of contact for young models who needed help to get out of the cycle. He did it pretty much single-handedly at the start—funded it all himself, took all the calls on his own mobile, twenty-four hours a day,' she said with proprietary pride. 'But typically he never talks about it.'

They were going down the stairs now and, suddenly light-headed, Eve had to grasp the banister for support.

So that was it. Ellie had had Raphael's number scribbled on the scrap of paper in her pocket not because he was a source of drugs, but of help.

Exhilaration flooded through her, as if her blood had been replaced with champagne. Stopping in the middle of the staircase, Eve turned to a bewildered Alessandra and, grinning broadly, said, *'Thank you.'*

Raphael was standing at the foot of the stairs, the light from the chandelier falling onto his broad, straight shoulders and glossy black hair. She wanted to jump down the last four stairs into his arms and kiss the life out of him. She wanted so, *so* much, and suddenly it all seemed possible.

He looked up as they approached, frowning slightly.

'I've neglected you all evening. I'm sorry.'

'I thought we weren't going to say sorry to each other any more?' she said, trying to suppress an absurdly big smile.

Alessandra hovered, looking stony beneath heavily applied lipstick. Placing a hand on Raphael's arm, she darted an accusing look at Eve and said something to him in very rapid Italian.

Raphael's face gave nothing away. 'Well, you'll just have to manage without me I'm afraid, Alessandra,' he replied in English, then looked down at Eve with the faintest hint of a smile. 'Let's go.'

He made no move to touch her, but, walking across the wide hallway, Eve could feel the white-heat of his nearness like a caress.

Alessandra watched them go, and as they reached the door she spoke again in the same quick, incomprehensible Italian, her voice stiff with malice.

Raphael hesitated, then turned.

'Thanks for the advice, Alessandra. But for future reference I'd just like you to remember that if I want your opinion I'll ask for it.'

His quietly controlled tone sent shivers down Eve's spine. But that was nothing to the fireworks that exploded in her pelvis as he slid a protective arm around her shoulders.

Looking meditatively back at Alessandra, he added with quiet bitterness, 'And, though it's none of your business, I hadn't forgotten. I wish I could.'

CHAPTER ELEVEN

AN APRICOT moon was reflected in the canal as they came out into the night air. The ageless tranquillity of the scene was in sharp contrast to the frenzied pulse of excitement that beat inside Eve's veins at the prospect of being alone with Raphael. She was trembling.

'You're cold,' he said, and before she could protest he had slipped off his dinner jacket and draped it over her bare shoulders.

It still bore the warm imprint of his body and a faint trace of the lemony tang of his cologne, underlaid by a deeper sandalwood scent that was all his own.

She looked up at him. He had pulled his silk bow tie undone and opened the top two buttons of his shirt, and her eye was automatically drawn to the hollow of bronzed skin at the base of his throat.

'What did Alessandra say?'

'Alessandra has a talent for stating the blatantly obvious and dressing it up as a profound insight,' he commented drily. 'Which apparently in the world of PR makes her something of a genius. When it relates to my personal life it just makes her annoying.'

'Your personal life?'

'Yes. She thought it would be helpful to point out that you're considerably younger than me.' He wasn't going to mention that she had also spitefully reminded him of Eve's profession. 'She's jealous.'

'Of me? Why?'

As she spoke she stumbled slightly on a cracked paving stone. With lightning swiftness Raphael had reached out and caught her. For a second he held her, looking down into her upturned face. The light from the streetlamp above them turned her blonde hair to silver.

'Now who's fishing for compliments?' he said with a small half-smile.

He let her go and she bent to take off the pink satin shoes with their unfamiliar high heels. As she stood up his jacket slipped off one creamy shoulder, and the harsh streetlight illuminated a crescent-shaped bruise on the side of her neck. Frowning, he brushed his thumb over it.

'How did you do this?'

She bit her lip and glanced down at her bare feet, then back up at him. Just like the first time he had spoken to her, at the retrospective party, her expression was sweet and gentle, but spiked with a hint of amusement.

'*I* didn't, exactly…'

He gave a soft moan and raked his fingers through his hair, remembering how he had buried his face in her neck as their lovemaking had reached its climax.

'*Dio*, Eve I'm s—'

She silenced him with a butterfly-light kiss. 'No apologies, remember?'

'If you do that again,' he growled, 'I'll be apologising to the magistrate in the morning for committing an act of public indecency.'

Pulling away, she took his hand and drew him forward. Enveloped by his jacket, she looked delicate, elfin and very mischievous.

'In that case we'd better hurry. I'd much rather commit an act of private indecency. Preferably more than one, in fact.'

He raised an eyebrow. 'It seems I have corrupted you.'

She turned, giving him a look of such scalding sexuality that he felt his body stiffen in instant response. Sparks of white heat glinted in the depths of her aquamarine eyes as she stood on the tiptoes of her bare brown feet and brushed her lips against his ear.

'Corrupted? No. You have *awakened* me.' Her mouth found his and gently, teasingly, her pink tongue darted between his parted lips. 'And for that I am truly grateful,' she finished in a breathy whisper that sent the blood rushing to his loins.

'So am I,' he murmured, sliding a hand into the front of her dress. 'So am I.'

The match flared in the darkness, illuminating the angular planes of Raphael's face as he held it to the candles in the Murano glass candelabra on the dressing table.

A flickering light spread its gentle fingers into the dark corners of the room, each of the six bright pillars reflected in the dull, silvered glass of the old mirror.

'Come back to bed.'

Eve's voice was sleepy and muffled by pillows as she lay face down in the tangle of bedclothes. The candlelight fell on the golden strands in her dark blonde hair and made her skin look almost luminescent against the stark white linen of the rumpled sheets.

'Don't move.'

'Hmm?'

'Don't move. I have to photograph you like that… You look like something from a religious painting in this light. The original Eve before the Fall—'

'Raphael?' she interrupted gently.

'What?'

'Shut up and get over here, *right now*.'

He laughed softly. 'You can't be wanting more already?' Propping himself up on one elbow beside her, he dropped a kiss into the little hollow at the base of her spine. Her seemingly insatiable passion both surprised and amused him.

'Can't I?'

He fell back onto the pillows, giving a theatrical moan. 'I told you I was too old…'

She flipped over onto her back so she could see him properly. 'Don't you dare start all that again!'

'No? What will you do?'

In a flash she was on top of him, her eyes glinting in the gentle candleglow.

'I'll just have to prove to you that you're not….' She gave a low, wicked laugh. 'Which shouldn't be too difficult as I have some *very* hard evidence right in front of me. Or should that be right underneath me?'

Sliding down the length of his thighs, she heard his fierce gasp as she took the smooth head of his erection into her mouth and moved her tongue languidly across its silken tip. She didn't stop to worry about whether she was doing it right, finding herself absolutely in the thrall of an irresistible, primitive instinct, guided by her own sensual pleasure.

She had never dreamed that bringing pleasure to a man would have this utterly explosive effect on her own desire. Closing her eyes in delirious ecstasy, she felt his hands grasping at her hair and found herself drenched with hot, urgent excitement.

'Now you, *cara*,' he rasped. 'Or, so help me, I won't be able to stop…'

Lifting her easily, he laid her down on the pillows. For a second she glimpsed the barely concealed need glittering in his dark eyes before he bent his head to kiss her collarbone, her breast, her belly button. She could feel the faint rasp of stubble on her quivering, sensitised skin as his mouth moved down the flat plane of her stomach, his tongue tip tracing a meandering path of ecstasy and anticipation. A deep moan of pleasure escaped him as he found the hot, wet triangle at the top of her thighs and he breathed in her hopelessly intoxicating natural perfume.

Her orgasm was swift and savage, and for a moment he wondered if he had hurt her. Gathering her into his arms, he held her until the waves that rippled through her tense body receded, leaving her languid and heavy.

'Raphael… Oh…'

She could feel the pressure of his arousal against her belly, and as she kissed him she tasted herself upon his lips.

Hardly moving her mouth from his, she murmured, *'More.'*

And this time he made sure it was slow and gentle and everything he had been too carried away to make it before. They didn't take their eyes off each other as, with every deep, deliberate thrust, they moved closer to their shared heaven. At the last moment he threw his head back and let go.

When he looked down at her again, tears were streaming down her cheeks. In the candlelight they looked like rivers of gold.

'You're up.'

Opening one azure eye and peeking out from underneath a tousled mass of silky hair, Eve gave a little mew of disappointment.

'And dressed. Very dressed.'

'I brought you some coffee.'

Eve wrinkled her nose.

'Bleugh… Tea?' she croaked pleadingly.

'Sorry. You won't find tea in many Italian kitchens—and here we run on the bare essentials. Coffee will have to do.'

He set it down on the little Victorian bedside table and walked over to the window, thrusting a hand through his hair to prevent himself from touching her. She had slept tucked into his body, but had now turned over onto her front again, and the honeyed length of her back was enticingly exposed. She looked utterly bloody irresistible, and it was going to take every ounce of self-control he possessed to get out of the *palazzo* and keep his appointment with Catalina.

Sleepily she rolled over and sat up, pulling the sheet over her breasts. Which was just as well, he thought grimly. The brief glimpse he'd just had of them was having an extremely profound effect on him.

'Where are you going?'

Her clear blue eyes regarded him steadily over the rim of her coffee cup and he had to turn away as he said, 'Out to meet someone. I told you last night, remember? It's business, but I'm afraid it's pretty important—or I wouldn't go.'

'I remember lots about last night, but that part had slipped my mind. I can't think why. Will you be long?'

He sighed heavily. 'Look, Eve, I have no idea. It could be over very quickly, it might take most of the day. I wish I could say—'

'Perhaps I should stay in bed, then,' she murmured with a mischievous smile. 'Just in case it is over very quickly. It would be silly to waste precious time getting dressed...'

She wasn't making this any easier. The look she was giving him was enough to bring him to his knees with longing, and he could feel the insistent pulse in his groin growing stronger by the second. Another five minutes and he wouldn't be leaving the *palazzo* for hours.

'Finish your article, there's a good girl. You can show it to me when I get back. There's bread and fruit down in the kitchen. Help yourself if you're hungry.'

All too aware of the delights concealed by the thin linen sheet, he didn't dare risk a kiss, and strode towards the door without a backward glance.

In the words of the song, what a difference a day made, Eve thought later, as she typed the final sentence of her article with a flourish. This time yesterday she'd been so miserable she hadn't been able to string a decent sentence together, and yet this morning the words flowed out of her fingertips in long, unbroken ribbons.

There was nothing to this journalism lark, she thought airily as she clicked 'word count'. Hurrah. Just a sliver under two thousand, spell-checked, and waiting to be e-mailed to Marissa Fox.

Humming quietly to herself, she set her laptop aside and got out of bed, stretching her cramped legs. She'd been a little cold after Raphael had left, so she'd slipped on the shirt he had worn last night, happily breathing in the scent of him on the crisp cotton as she'd worked, letting the images it evoked float sensually around in her mind. He was so…sexy, she thought with a little shiver, marvelling at her reflection in the dressing table mirror. She looked wickedly, *glowingly* exhausted.

She giggled. Perhaps *Glitterati* would be interested in an article entitled 'Sex: the new Botox'.

Picking up her mobile, she sent Lou a hasty text message.

In Venice with R. Article finished…

She hesitated, smiling to herself as she considered adding *virginity also*. Lou had been on at her for what seemed like for ever about getting rid of it on anyone—almost as if it were some sort of unwanted Christmas gift. How glad she was now that she hadn't. No one else could have introduced her to the pleasures of the bedroom with a millionth of the passion and tender expertise of Raphael. She felt her heart skip a beat at the memory.

Everything OK, she finished lamely. It seemed a totally inadequate way to sum up the utter euphoria she was feeling, but Lou would see that for herself when Eve returned to London.

Joyfully she clasped the phone to her chest and twirled around. *If* she returned to London. Being separated from Raphael for a few hours today was bad enough, and the thought of being apart from him for any longer was appalling.

Suddenly deflated, she collapsed onto the bed and expelled a long breath.

That attitude was neither healthy nor attractive, and she had always had a strong disdain for clingy women. Come to think of it, this morning he'd seemed a little cold and distant, so she must be careful not to irritate him with suffocating adoration.

Outside the ancient windows of the *palazzo* Venice glittered in the summer sunshine—while she waited in the bedroom like some drippy girlfriend.

Purposefully she got up. No more lovesick mooning. She would go and explore.

Within minutes of leaving the *palazzo* Eve was lost.

She'd thought she knew the way to Piazza San Marco, but after wandering through two narrow and unfamiliar *calles* she had to admit that she was wrong. Each time she had been with Raphael, she acknowledged with a shiver of remembrance, her mind had been on other things.

She could still see the distinctive bell tower of Saint Mark's ahead of her, above the jumbled rooftops, but instead of getting closer to it she seemed to be getting further away.

She'd intended to make her way back to Saint Mark's Square and maybe take a photo of the basilica on her phone to send to Lou, and prove that she really was in Venice. Instead she found herself wandering further and further off the beaten track. The little passageways were filled with the smell of frying garlic from the kitchens of tiny *trattoria* frequented only by locals. Eve's stomach rumbled, reminding her that she hadn't done as Raphael had instructed and made herself some breakfast at the *palazzo*. She had discovered the dingy, old-fashioned kitchen and retreated hastily, preferring to find a café.

Although for the first time in her life she wasn't craving chocolate.

This really must be love.

She crossed a little bridge, nodded politely at an old woman coming the other way, and paused before entering a narrow passageway between two tall, crumbling buildings. It smelt suffocatingly of damp and decay, and she found her heart was beating so hard that she feared the sound must be echoing off the high walls above her. She hesitated, wondering whether to retrace her steps and ask the old woman for directions, but pride and her inadequate Italian prevented her. Quickening her pace, she walked on.

The passageway opened out into a small, sunlit square with a café at the far end. The *campanile* was to the right of her now, so she must have come almost full circle and now be heading back in the direction of St Mark's. She breathed a grateful sigh of relief, and was just wondering whether to stop and order some tea or keep going when the blood seemed to freeze in her veins.

For a second she thought she was going to faint. Blackness blocked out the sun, and blindly she stretched a hand out behind her, groping for the support of a wall to lean on. Gradually her vision cleared, and she was able to see for certain that her first glance had been horribly, sickeningly accurate.

Raphael was leaning across a table, clasping the hands of a fragile-looking dark-haired woman. He had his back towards her, but there was no mistaking the deep indigo linen shirt, the sharply slanting sweep of cheekbone that was all she could see of his face beneath the dark hair. And, she realised with another sickening lurch of her stomach, there was no mistaking his intimacy with the woman opposite him. Holding both her hands between both of his, he was leaning towards her, speaking intently to her. There was no way this was a casual encounter with an old acquaintance.

Or a business meeting.

And then, in front of Eve's horrified eyes, he half rose from his seat and took the woman's face in his hands to press a kiss onto her trembling mouth.

Clapping her hand to her mouth, to try and stifle the terrible sobs that threatened to tear her apart, Eve turned on her heel and ran.

* * *

'Don't ask me to do this, Raphael, *please*!'

Raphael tightened his grip on Catalina's hands.

'I wouldn't if I had any other way of getting Luca locked up. You're our only chance, Cat. You said yourself that most of the other girls who've fallen into his clutches are either lost in the drugs underworld and wouldn't be reliable witnesses or are dead. Like your friend—Ellie, was it? You'd be given absolute protection and treated with complete respect. I promise.'

He felt some of the fight go out of her.

'I trust you Raphael. *Va bene*,' she whispered.

'You'll do it?'

'*Si*, I'll try.'

Almost dizzy with relief, Raphael felt like leaping up and doing a victory dance around the square, but he settled instead for stretching across the table and giving her a quick kiss of pure gratitude. As he sat down again he saw the colour drain from her cheeks and an expression of utter terror come over her face. Wide-eyed and ashen-faced she leapt to her feet, almost over-turning the table as she stared at a spot just over his shoulder.

Instantly Raphael was beside her, taking her in his arms.

'Cat? Cat! What's wrong? What's the matter?'

She pointed a shaking finger across the square. 'She was there! She was! She looked at me!'

Raphael glanced over his shoulder.

'Who?'

'Ellie!'

'Ellie? Your friend who died?'

Catalina nodded, burying her face in Raphael's shoulder and sobbing brokenly. Automatically Raphael patted her back, making soft sounds of comfort while his mind raced.

He knew all about the hallucinations that were an after-effect of addiction. *Damn*. Talking about the past had probably triggered something off. She clearly wasn't as together as he'd first thought.

'There's no one there, Cat. Shh… There's no one there. Come on, *cara*, let's get you home.'

Grimly he pulled some money from his pocket and left it on the table, then took the arm of a sobbing, incoherent Catalina.

The tantalising image of Eve in bed at the *palazzo* taunted him, and he cursed inwardly. It looked as if this was going to take a while, after all.

CHAPTER TWELVE

BLINDED by her tears, Eve continued to run, without hesitating to think where she was going. Dimly she was aware of going back over the bridge she had crossed only minutes before. But that seemed like a different lifetime. She was almost surprised to see the same old woman, only a short way along the canalside from the bridge. How could everything else be so absurdly normal when her world had just collapsed about her ears?

Eventually a stabbing pain in her side forced her to stop running, and she sank down in a doorway and wept.

No wonder Raphael had seemed so uptight this morning. And no wonder he had been so vague about when he would be back. With another flood of anguish she remembered his impatience as he'd said—what was it?—*It could be over very quickly; it might take most of the day.* This woman must be an old flame he had been hoping to rekindle, and he hadn't been sure what kind of reception he'd get.

Well, he certainly seemed to have lucked out, Eve thought savagely. From the way he'd leaned over and kissed her it didn't look as if he was going to be heading back to the *palazzo* any time soon.

She'd been so *stupid*. Stupid and naïve. Right from the moment they had first set eyes on each other she had thought that the feelings that existed between herself and Raphael were rare and extraordinary. She had been so overwhelmed by their power that she'd put herself in a position of potential danger to be with him, and her discovery last night that he wasn't what she'd thought had been a moment of pure joy.

Well, he might not be a drug pushing low-life, but he was a two-timing liar. And the way she felt now, that was just about as bad as it got.

'Eve? Eve, *cara*, I thought it was you! *Tesoro*, what is wrong?'

'Luca! Oh, Luca… How did you…?'

'My hotel is over there. Oh, *bambino*, tell me—what has made you cry?'

Next moment she was in his arms, her head buried in his shoulder as she wept. He smelled of cigarettes and booze, and she found herself thinking that it was a far cry from Raphael's clean, lemony tang, but he was familiar, and he was here—and for that she was immensely grateful.

Gently he held her away from him and peered into her face. 'Shh, *cara*, shh. It is Raphael, no?'

She nodded dumbly.

'Is he hurt?'

There was something slightly wild in Luca's eyes, and he shook her by the shoulder a little as he asked the question again. Taking deep, shuddering breaths Eve managed to shake her head again.

'I saw him with…with…another woman. In a café. He was…' For a moment tears choked her again, and she gratefully took the handkerchief that Luca offered her. After blowing her nose she continued, struggling to keep calm. 'They were holding hands. And then he kissed her.'

Luca gave a low whistle. 'What did she look like, this woman?'

Eve shrugged dejectedly. 'Long dark hair, very slim… I don't know. Kind of fragile-looking, I suppose. Like an anorexic version of Alessandra.'

Luca's eyes glittered and he looked oddly pleased. 'Catalina.'

'You know her?' Eve wailed.

'*Si*. She and Raphael had a big thing a few years ago, when she was modelling for Lazaro. But wait, *cara*,' he said soothingly, as Eve started a fresh bout of sobbing, 'it was all over a long time ago. I can't imagine for a minute that Raphael would want her back *now*.'

'Wh-why n-not?' Eve gulped. She didn't like the tone of Luca's voice.

'Because she is damaged goods, *cara*, that is why. Drink, drugs and a whole lot of depravity have taken their toll. Believe me, I speak as one who knows. She has most definitely lost her youthful sparkle.' He smiled nastily and stroked a finger down Eve's cheek. 'Unlike you, *mio carino*. Come—I know where Catalina's apartment is. Let us go there and—'

'No! I couldn't! I don't want to see them!'

'Calm down, *bambino*, calm down. You are jumping to conclusions. We'll go there, and I bet we find Catalina alone. You will meet her and you'll see what I mean about her. Then you will go back to Raphael and give him big kiss and tell him how silly you are. Yes?'

Eve scrubbed at her cheeks with the handkerchief, feeling the tiniest glimmer of optimism. If Luca thought she was being silly, maybe she was.

'OK.'

'*Bene*. Let's go.'

'Nearly there, *cara*. Catalina's *appartemente* is in that building there, on the first floor.'

Eve followed his gaze. Like many of Venice's buildings, the one he pointed out was painted a soft shade of ochre, and in spite of the fact that the paint was peeling and the stonework flaking it had about in an air of faded grandeur. The three storeys above street level were each dominated by tall, elegant windows, some of which opened onto tiny balconies, and the huge door to the building was set into an elaborate stone frame. The whole impression was of a building where important things had happened over the centuries.

Eve just hoped nothing important was going on there now.

Her footsteps slowed as they approached, until Luca was virtually dragging her along. She stopped altogether as they drew level with the building.

And then she saw them.

'No,' she rasped, staring up in disbelief. 'Oh, God… Luca, look. In the window.'

For a moment Luca didn't speak, and in awful fascination they watched Raphael unbutton Catalina's dress, then kiss her forehead.

'I'm sorry, *bambino*, so sorry. It seems you were right,' Luca murmured.

He had to force her to turn away, but by that time she had already seen Raphael lower the bedroom blind. Tears were coursing silently down her cheeks as Luca led her briskly back the way they had come.

After receiving the news of Ellie's death Eve remembered the curious feeling of numbness that had come over her. Everyone around her had treated her with the utmost gentleness, as if she were an intricate and unstable piece of finely tuned machinery that they were afraid of breaking. She hadn't been able to cry.

She wished for a little of that numbness now. All she wanted to do was scream and rage and beat her fists on the floor, like a child having a tantrum in a toyshop. *I want Raphael, I want Raphael! It's not fair!*

Going back to the *palazzo* was a particularly cruel torture. In a daze, Eve climbed the stairs which Raphael had carried her up only twenty-four hours previously.

'Which room?'

'Sorry?'

Luca rolled his eyes. 'Which room are your things in? You forget, *cara*, this is Isabella's palazzo. I have never been allowed inside it before. I do not know my way around.'

'Here.'

It seemed incredible that everything looked just the same as when she had left it just a couple of hours ago. The unmade bed—the scene of such joy and passion—seemed to mock her, and throwing herself down upon it she buried her face in the rumpled sheets, breathing in the lingering scent of sex and Raphael.

'Come on, *bella*, don't cry.'

She knew she was beginning to frustrate Luca, but she didn't care. His initial tenderness was starting to give way to a restlessness that frightened her a little.

'Your bag? Where is it?'

'I'm not sure. Raphael put it…' She bit her lip against another surge of tears. 'There it is—under the bed. I don't have much else.'

The pale green dress was draped carefully over the back of a little chair, and Eve went over and stroked the satiny material. She had been so happy when she'd worn it. Now she felt exactly as the dress looked—empty and forlorn. As far as Raphael was concerned she was yesterday's news, something to be tidied away when she was no longer required.

'Ready?'

Eve nodded, but didn't turn round. Behind her, Luca's voice was sharp with impatience. 'Come, then. We must return to my hotel to collect my bags first, then we go to Marco Polo. I have ordered that the jet be made ready.'

She looked round, wide-eyed with alarm 'Not the Lazaro jet?'

'*Si, cara.* I may not have been allowed in here before, but you forget—I am a di Lazaro too.'

'But I can't—'

She stopped, aware of how ridiculous it would sound. *I can't bear the thought of it without him.*

Luca's voice was smooth and dangerous.

'I think you can, *bambino*. Unless you want to stay here. Perhaps you would enjoy a little *ménage à trois* with Raphael and Catalina?' He laughed unpleasantly at his own joke, then, seeing her stricken face, put an arm around her trembling shoulders.

'Don't worry, *bella*. Luca will look after you. And if you are a very good girl I will give you something nice to help you relax.'

'What do you mean?'

He grinned and tapped the side of his nose mysteriously. 'I show you later. Now, let's get out of this place. It gives me the creeps.'

'I love it,' said Eve fiercely. She shut the bedroom door and leaned her head against it for a second as tears seeped out from beneath her closed eyelids. The image of the unmade bed was firmly imprinted in the darkness in her head, and she suspected it would stay there for a very long time to come: the scene of such brief but perfect happiness.

It was halfway through the afternoon when Raphael finally let himself into the *palazzo*. He carried a large box of English breakfast tea that he'd bought at a vastly inflated price from the owner of a smart café he'd passed on the way back from Catalina's apartment.

He had left Catalina sleeping deeply, having had to undress her as if she were a child and put her to bed. Getting her home from the café had plumbed reserves of patience and strength he hadn't known he possessed, as she had screamed and sobbed, saying the name of the dead girl over and over again. *Ellie*.

Raphael stopped just inside the doorway of the *palazzo*, his brows drawn together in an agonised frown. He'd sunk everything he'd got into setting up the helpline for girls like her— Catalina said she had even had the number—but it still hadn't been enough to compete with the ruthlessness of Luca.

He'd waited until Catalina's mother had arrived before leaving the apartment, and had spoken to Signora Di Souza at some length about the possibility of Catalina giving evidence against Luca. It had been a huge relief to find that she was in favour of the idea. Together, they'd agreed, they would give her the support she needed to brave the witness box if and when the case came to trial. For the first time Raphael had allowed himself to cautiously believe that it really was a case of when. He would ring Marco immediately.

Taking the stairs two at a time, he felt his mouth curve into a smile. Well, maybe not immediately…

Quietly he opened the door, wondering if Eve had been true to her word and stayed in bed. After all, they hadn't had much sleep last night.

'Eve?'

The room was empty, and there was something about the emptiness that sent a shiver right through him. With a casualness he didn't feel he tossed aside the box of tea and sauntered over to look underneath the bed, where he had stowed their bags.

His was there. Roughly he pulled it out of the way, desperate to find hers hidden behind it.

Nothing.

He stood up and looked wildly around. Snatching the mobile phone from his pocket with shaking hands, he scrolled through in search of the number for Marco Polo airport.

Five minutes later, having ascertained there was no one with the name of Eve Middlemiss booked onto any of the outward flights that day, he allowed himself to breathe a little easier, and sank onto the bed with a groan of despair. If she was still on the island she must have checked into a hotel, for some crazy reason. Which meant he had a lot of calls to make.

Just as he was about to begin, the phone in his hand started to ring.

'*Pronto?*'

'Signor di Lazaro? It's Roberto. I thought I should let you know Signor Luca has just boarded the jet back to Florence.' There was a small pause, then Roberto said more quietly, 'He has with him Signorina Middlemiss.'

Raphael let out a vicious expletive. 'Are you in the air yet?'

'No, *signore*, but Signor Luca is in a hurry to leave. We will be taking off in a few minutes.'

'Thanks for letting me know, Roberto.'

'*Ne problemo, signore.* Would you like us to fly back for you once we've dropped Signor Luca at Amerigo Vespucci?'

'*Si, per favore.* Let me know when you can get airspace.'

'Of course, *signore.*'

'Oh, and Roberto…?' Raphael pressed a shaking hand to his forehead. 'Could you ask Nico to keep a very close eye on Signorina Middlemiss, please? She…she doesn't enjoy take-off very much. Look after her for me.'

White-lipped, Raphael let the phone fall from his hand onto the unmade bed, then walked over to the window. This was where he had stood yesterday, just after they'd made love. Just twenty-four short hours ago. Closing his eyes, he could picture it exactly. Eve had sat on the bed in that dress, her beautiful face softened with compassion and tenderness, as he'd talked about his mother's death. Her eyes had been alight with love. And he'd been too bloody stupid to see it.

He clenched his fists and pressed them against the glass. *No! Be honest with yourself!*

He'd seen it. He'd just been too bitter and screwed-up and suspicious to admit he felt it too. He'd tried to tell himself Eve was just doing her job.

'*Dio!*' His voice was a cry of anguish in the ghost-filled room. For how long had he been using his own cynical, emotionally sterile standards to judge everyone else? He remembered how bitterly he'd berated his father, his damning words coming back to haunt him mockingly: *If he'd loved her he would have protected her…*

He'd been wrong about everything.

He loved Eve, and it didn't make him able to protect her. It just gave him greater power to hurt her.

Frantically throwing clothes into his bag, he just hoped it wasn't too late to say sorry.

* * *

The streets of Florence were deserted as Raphael drove through them in the early hours, jumping red lights and screeching round corners far too fast. He didn't care if he was pulled over by the *polizia*. Marco would vouch for him.

As he got nearer to Luca's flat he began to feel almost light-headed with adrenalin and lack of sleep. Every fibre of his body thrummed, and each minute that passed was like a knife-edge on his frayed nerves.

If Luca had laid one finger on Eve…

He had spent the entire crucifyingly slow journey from Venice thinking about exactly what he would do. And it wasn't pleasant.

This was it. Abandoning his car on the double yellow lines outside Luca's building, he pressed the buzzer and waited for the concierge. He had had plenty of time to work out his line on the plane.

'Raphael Di Lazaro. I'm afraid I need to see my brother urgently. Our father…'

Instantly the concierge opened the door, ushering Raphael in with compassionate haste. He had been reading all about Antonio's illness in the newspaper he had hastily folded under his desk, and wasted no time in offering his sympathy.

'*Grazie*. I'm sorry—I'm still a little shocked—which *appartemente* is my brother's?'

'The penthouse, *signore*.'

Raphael concealed a grimace. He should have guessed Luca would occupy the flashiest apartment in the building.

The lift seemed to take an eternity as it climbed to the top floor. In the greenish tinted mirrors Raphael hardly recognised his own face. He seemed to have aged twenty years in the last twenty hours—which was roughly the time since he'd last seen Eve. Stubble darkened his jaw, and his eyes were almost as shadowed and hollow as Catalina's. He was still wearing the blue shirt that she'd soaked with her tears, he thought in distaste, remembering the dry, feverish heat of her thin body as he'd tried to console her. Eve's cool freshness seemed as remote and unreachable as a waterfall in a desert.

Please, God, let her be there.

The lift doors opened. There was only one door in the small, tastefully bland hallway.

When Luca opened it Raphael experienced a small twinge of surprise that he was fully dressed. An unpleasant smile spread slowly across his face when he saw Raphael.

'Raphael—how good of you to drop in and see me! It's rather a strange hour for a social call, though, wouldn't you say?'

Pushing him roughly aside, Raphael strode into the apartment and started opening doors. 'Where is she?'

'I'm sorry—who?'

'Eve.' He said it like a snarl, not knowing how long he could hang on to his last shreds of self-control.

'Ah! The delightful Eve! I'm afraid you've missed her. By now she'll be just about—' he checked his watch '—touching down at Heathrow, I should imagine. We only stopped off here to kill a few hours before her flight.' His greasy laugh sent a fresh surge of adrenalin pumping through Raphael's body. 'But I'm very glad we did! I guess I have to thank you, big brother—you broke her in beautifully!'

White-faced, Raphael turned back to Luca. 'I don't believe you.'

'What? That she's flying back to London right now?' Luca said with exaggerated innocence. 'Would you like to call the British Airways check-in desk? I can't remember the flight number, exactly, but—'

'Oh, I'll check she was on it, believe me. Although I admit there's a chance that you're telling the truth about *that*.'

'Ah, so the bit you don't believe is that Eve was keen to practise her new-found skills on me?' Luca looked suddenly incredibly pleased with himself, like a magician the moment before he pulls a rabbit out of a hat in front of an eager audience. 'Well, since you did so much of the groundwork, perhaps you deserve to see the photographs.'

For a second Raphael seriously thought he was in danger of passing out as Luca held out a fan of five or six Polaroid snaps of a blonde girl. In the top one she was reclining on a bed, naked except for black stockings and stiletto-heeled shoes.

It was Eve.

'They're not up to your standard, I know, but rather nice—'

The next moment there was a sickening thud and the unmistakable snap of bone as Raphael's fist smashed into Luca's face and he fell backwards against the open door of the apartment. Stepping over his crumpled body, Raphael didn't even look down. It was only as the lift carried him back down to the ground floor that he noticed his hand was wet with blood.

CHAPTER THIRTEEN

London. Six months later.

'AND so she was wondering if you'd like to do an article on it. What do you think? Eve? *Eve!*'

Eve dragged her gaze away from the couple in the corner of the sandwich bar and back to Lou, who was looking at her sternly.

'Sorry—what was that?'

'Marissa. She was wondering whether you'd do a couple of thousand words on single pregnancy for the magazine. It struck us that there's been loads written about actually being a single mum, but not much about going through a pregnancy alone.'

'Probably because most people actually manage to stay with their partner for at least nine months,' muttered Eve gloomily.

Lou took no notice. 'You take the starting point of doing the test—you know, mixed feelings and so on—who do you tell first?—right through to how you choose a birth partner.' She beamed. 'Of course, *I* hope to feature in this article pretty heavily…'

Eve took a sip of her tea, hoping it would dislodge the familiar lump in her throat that signalled the onset of tears. Again. Who would have thought she could still have any tears left?

'It would be quite a positive piece, you see. There's really nothing that a partner does that your best friend or a health professional can't. And maybe does better.'

Eve squeezed her eyes shut for a second. *What about telling you how beautiful you are with that particular fierce sincerity? What about holding you and talking to you in the middle of the night when you can't sleep?*

The man at the table in the corner reached across and smoothed a strand of hair back from the girl's face. In the warm fug of the little sandwich bar he had taken off his outdoor coat to reveal a blue shirt, and though his dark hair was neatly cropped, and his face was much less arresting, he still reminded her of Raphael.

But then, somehow or other, most things did.

At that moment the baby gave a little jump, and Eve's hand fluttered to her belly. No doubt Raphael hadn't given her a moment's thought since he'd returned to the *palazzo* that day and found her gone, but, for Eve, forgetting him just wasn't going to be an option. Ever.

'So you'll do it, won't you? The deadline for copy is a week on Wednesday.'

'I can't.'

Lou almost choked on her latte. 'Eve, you must! This is a great opportunity to earn a bit of extra cash before the baby's born and reach out to other women going through the same thing. OK, forget the positive angle and say how difficult it's been—how you worry that your unhappiness during pregnancy might have somehow affected the baby, how you wonder what to tell it about its father as it grows up.'

'Sorry, Lou. I really can't. I had a letter this morning about giving evidence at Luca di Lazaro's trial. I'm flying out on Monday.'

'Oh, God. You should have said.'

'They're still not completely sure that they're going to use me—and if they do when it'll be—but the prosecution want me to be on hand just in case.'

'Will you be giving evidence about Ellie?'

Eve shrugged, making little dark stars out of a splash of

coffee on the table with the end of a spoon. 'I don't know. I've sent the barrister those photographs Ellie sent me from Florence, of her on the steps of the Uffizi, so they can match them up to some pretty lurid photographs they found in Luca's flat. But they might want me to give evidence about what happened on the journey back from Venice—the stuff I told the police about at the time.'

Lou's eyes were round with dismay. 'Oh, no, Eve… You can't go through all that again. Not in your condition! Do they know you're pregnant?'

'No, but it makes no difference. I've got to do this—for Ellie's sake more than mine. I mean, it's not as if he actually harmed me in any way on the jet. After he pulled his little stunt I made sure we weren't alone for a second.'

'No, but you were still an absolute wreck when you got home.'

Eve sighed. 'I know, I know. But that wasn't entirely down to Luca. He only offered me a line of cocaine—'

'Blimey, Eve, you make it sound like a cup of tea!'

'No—I mean, I was shocked and everything, and his aggression when I refused scared me a bit, but Nico—the steward—was there, and I knew he would make sure I was safe. I must admit it was a horrible, horrible moment when he said that he'd known Ellie and I realised that *he* must have been her supplier, but…well, I was a wreck before I even got on the plane with him.'

No change there, then, she added mentally, suspecting Lou was thinking exactly the same thing. She had been enormously supportive throughout the appalling trauma of Eve finding out she was pregnant, but six months down the line her willingness to hand out a constant supply of tissues was starting to wane. Eve couldn't blame her.

'So, will *he* be in court too?'

'Who?'

'Who do you think? *Raphael*, of course.'

'I don't know.' She hadn't dared ask Marco. 'I hope not.'

'Well, I bloody well hope he is, and that his new girlfriend can see exactly what kind of bastard he is! The kind who seduces young girls and gets them pregnant, then buggers off without another word.'

Eve winced and looked down into the dregs of her tea. 'Not quite without another word. He did call the magazine…'

'Yeah—great,' said Lou with blistering sarcasm. 'What was that message again? *Tell her I'm sorry. She'll understand. Make sure she has my number.* Nice one, Romeo. Like she's *really* going to call!'

'Don't,' whispered Eve.

'Well, honestly! *She'll understand.* Understand what? That he just had to distribute his virile Italian charms fairly amongst the female population? It would be petty of any girl to object to that, wouldn't it?'

A fat tear slid out from under Eve's glasses and dripped into her cup. Noticing it, Lou was instantly contrite.

'God, Eve, I'm sorry. I didn't mean to upset you. I just hate the thought of you having to face that bastard again.'

'I'll be fine,' Eve replied unconvincingly, removing her glasses to wipe her eyes with a paper napkin.

'I'll come with you.'

Eve gave her a watery smile, touched by the determination in Lou's voice. Her sympathy might be wearing thin, but her loyalty never failed.

'Don't be silly. I've had enough trouble getting time off from *my* work at such short notice. Marissa would hit the roof. And I don't know how long I'll be there or anything.'

'Well, I'll phone every day. At least three times,' Lou conceded reluctantly. 'Someone's got to remind you to take your iron supplement.'

* * *

Raphael emerged from the court building and stood for a moment breathing in the damp air of the winter evening. Rain was falling steadily on the street-lit pavement, and he threw back his head and let it wet his face. It had been a long, gruelling day.

It was Catalina's first day in the witness box, and she hadn't coped well. Bit by bit the defence barrister was undermining her confidence, making her version of events seem more and more shaky by the hour. It was exactly what she had been afraid of.

It was also exactly what Gianni Orseolo, the prosecution barrister, had feared.

Appearing in the doorway of the building, Gianni shook out a huge purple and green umbrella emblazoned with the gold logo of his polo club and came over to Raphael.

'Are you walking this way? Good. Not a great day, I think you'll agree. They're tearing her to shreds out there. I'm calling a new witness tomorrow. Catalina won't stand up to any further questioning.'

They watched a grey-faced Catalina being led out of court by her parents, a sight that left them both subdued.

'*Bene,*' said Raphael curtly. 'I think I may stay away tomorrow. I'm not sure I can stand another day of looking at Luca's smug face, and I ought to go and see my father.'

'Well, unless it's urgent I recommend you put it off for another day. Tomorrow's witness could make up some ground for us—it might be worth coming in to see Luca squirming in his seat. How is your father, by the way?'

'Until the trial started he was improving every day. Being back at the villa made a big difference. But all this has hit him hard. He adores Luca.'

Gianni Orseolo came from one of Florence's wealthiest families, and he and Raphael had known each other since they were boys. Not well enough to be in the habit of exchanging confidences, but there was something peculiarly intimate about their close proximity under the umbrella in the dark, rain-lashed street.

'The golden boy, eh? While you were the black sheep? And now Antonio has to shift his perspective a little.'

'And me too.' Raphael thrust his hands deep into the pockets of his long coat and looked out into the rain. 'I'd got very used to the idea of hating my father and blaming him for my mother's death. I… Someone…changed my perspective on that…'

At least that was one thing he had to thank Eve for. At least she had left a tiny glimmer of something good in the ruins of his life.

As always, he ruthlessly pushed the thought of her out of his mind.

'Families are complicated things,' Gianni agreed lightly, 'which is why, Raphael old friend, we are very wise in choosing to avoid that path ourselves.'

Raphael said nothing.

Gianni's car was easily recognisable amongst all the small city hatchbacks and family saloons parked along the street. Raphael gave a short bark of laughter as they approached the ridiculously predictable red Ferrari.

'Very nice, Gianni. Very practical.'

'It is for my purposes. As a young bachelor—' he smiled rakishly '—one has to invest in all the right equipment to attract the right ladies.' He pressed the keypad, setting off a volley of flashing lights on the dash, but just as he was about to stoop and open the impossibly streamlined door he turned thoughtfully back to Raphael.

'I know it's none of my business, but you look like you could do with a good night out.' That was a pretty huge understatement. Secretly Gianni was horrified by how gaunt Raphael appeared, almost as if it should be *he* who was in the dock for drugs crimes, not Luca. 'Look, I'm heading out of town at the weekend. Going to stay in the villa of an old mate with a few friends. You'd be more than welcome—it would do you good to get away from all this and have some fun. I've got the perfect girl—'

'No.' Raphael had left the shelter of the umbrella and was already walking away from Gianni along the darkened street.

'Dinner, then. You'd love this girl—'

Raphael shook his head. 'Thanks, Gianni, but no.'

'Can I at least give you a lift anywhere?'

Raphael had almost disappeared into the darkness, but his voice drifted back through the rain.

'*Grazie*, but I prefer to walk.'

Shaking his head in bewilderment, Gianni slid into the driver's seat and fired up the engine with a roar. If he didn't know Raphael better he'd say he looked like a man with a broken heart.

Raphael had got walking without thinking down to a fine art. Head down, oblivious to the rain, he cleared his mind of everything except the calming rhythm of his footsteps.

As soon as Luca's arrest had been secured he had taken his camera and headed back to Columbia. Not, this time, to the places and people with which he had become so familiar on previous trips, but to the mountains. The days he had spent there, just walking and photographing the landscape, had helped him come to terms with Eve's betrayal, even if they hadn't brought him any closer to understanding it.

Before he went he had called the magazine and left a message and a number. Not knowing what to say to the bored-sounding receptionist, he'd simply asked that she tell Eve he was sorry, hoping she would recognise and respond to the private meaning those words held for them both. When she didn't, he'd had to conclude that it and everything else that had happened between them had ultimately meant more to him than it had to her.

He hadn't been able to make sense of it, so, with his habitual ruthless self-control, he'd blanked it out. As a policy it probably wasn't conducive to long-term mental health and happiness, but he was prepared to take his chances.

The rain was falling harder than ever now, and he could feel it seeping under the upturned collar of his coat and trickling down his neck. Suddenly, with all the pain of a physical blow, he was reminded of Venice. Standing in Piazza San Marco as the storm broke…the fury that had burned in Eve's indescribably beautiful eyes which had turned so quickly to passion…

Gritting his teeth, he ground the key into the lock of his front door and threw it open, then slammed it shut behind him

When denial didn't work there was always anger.

Shaking the rain from his hair, he went along the passage-way to the kitchen and filled a jug with water for the coffee machine. It was the only item in the gleaming kitchen that looked even vaguely used. Signora Arrigo, Raphael's cleaner, worried endlessly about him, and lately had even taken to leaving portions of her home-made pasta or soup in the fridge. Today a small loaf of focaccia rested under a linen towel on the worktop.

Smiling wanly at her kindness, he opened the cupboard to get coffee, then paused. At the very back something caught his eye, and he reached in and pulled it out.

English breakfast tea.

How utterly pitiful he had become. Ridiculous enough that he'd brought it back to Florence in the first place—but as for keeping it for the past six desperate months… That was just deluded. What was he thinking? That one day she would turn up on his doorstep out of the blue? Offer to give him another chance over a cup of decent tea?

There was a loud crash as the packet of tea hit the wall and met its target in the sleek metal bin.

Snatching up a bottle of red wine, Raphael left the kitchen, all thoughts of food and coffee forgotten. His sitting room was on the first floor, and without bothering to switch the light on he went to stand at the window.

Outside, the rain looked like shoals of tiny silver fishes in the streetlights. Raphael took a long mouthful of wine, determinedly driving out the memories that crowded around the edges of his mind, insistent and enticing. Eve's head on his knee as they drove on the street down there. The softness of her hair under his hand. The warmth of her breath on his thigh…

It was the details that haunted him.

Giving a groan of despair, he turned away from the window and reached for the television remote control. News. Football. Anything so long as it offered some blissful respite from the endless torment of his own thoughts.

The screen showed a bare stage, with a Japanese-style paper screen as its backdrop. Raphael froze, rigid with disbelief, as the soprano began to sing and the hair-raisingly beautiful, spine-chillingly lonely aria filled the darkened room.

Madame Butterfly.

Pouring the remainder of the wine into his glass, he leaned his head back against the wall and closed his eyes. The pale light from the window showed exquisite agony on his stricken face.

CHAPTER FOURTEEN

FLORENCE in February was an entirely different city from the one Eve had left in August. A slick of rain darkened the elegant streets. Tourists huddled in waterproofed groups as they consulted their guidebooks, oblivious to the majesty of the buildings that towered above them.

Sitting behind the uncommunicative driver sent by Marco to take her from her hotel to the courtroom, Eve stared unseeingly out at the headlamps of the passing cars and tried not to think about Raphael.

She was shaking. Even the remote possibility of seeing him again was making her heart do things that didn't feel healthy, and she could imagine what her midwife would say if she took her blood pressure right now. For the sake of her sanity, and the health of her baby, she tried to keep her mind focused on Luca.

She was here to close the grim chapter that had started three years ago with Ellie's death. Her own small tragedy was incidental.

The car pulled up in front of a forbidding-looking building, and the driver got out and put up an umbrella before opening the door for her. For a moment he stood impassively, waiting for her to get out, but then, seeing the tears sliding down her pale cheeks, and noticing how much she was trembling, he quickly stepped forward and offered her his arm. He was younger than she'd realised, but his voice, when he spoke, was deep and comforting.

'Don't worry. Please don't cry.'

Gently he held her arm as she got out of the car, and helped her up the steps to the building. Eve felt that without his support her legs would simply give way beneath her.

Speaking in abrupt Italian into a small, hand-held radio, he guided her to a long marble-pillared corridor with benches on both sides, and motioned to her to take a seat.

Eve shook her head. Her back ached from sitting so tensely in the car, and she placed both hands at the base of her spine and flexed it slightly.

'*Caffe, signorina?*'

'No, *grazie*. I'm…'

The words died on her lips as she looked up. Footsteps were approaching from the other end of the corridor, brisk and businesslike, and adrenalin crashed through her like water through a burst dam as she found herself looking straight into the eyes that had haunted her dreams for six tortuous months.

Raphael's face was ghostly pale in the gloom, and the hollows beneath his cheekbones were as dark as if they had been painted on. But it was his eyes that held her attention. In the few brief moments before he disappeared ahead of her into the court room they burned into her with a ferocity that felt like hatred.

'Could you confirm your full name, please?'

Gianni Orseolo's voice was gentle, but still Eve could not suppress her violent trembling, nor look up and meet the eyes of the man seated beside the suave lawyer.

'Eve Maria Middlemiss.' Her voice was a cracked whisper in the sudden silence of the courtroom. She was aware of Luca, seated opposite her, with uniformed police on either side of him and stole a quick glance at him. His air of glossy, laughing insouciance had completely disappeared, and he was grey and tense. His face looked different too, though she couldn't work out why.

'Signorina Middlemiss—you are English, yes?' Eve gave a small nod. 'Can you tell the court when was the first time you travelled to Italy?'

'Last summer. In August.'

Gianni risked a gentle smile. 'Not, perhaps, a good time to catch Florence at its quietest,' he said gravely, and a ripple of laughter ran through the court. Then he was serious again. 'What was the purpose of your visit, *signorina?*'

'I was commissioned by a magazine to write an article on the Lazaro fashion retrospective. It was supposed to be a sort of behind-the-scenes kind of thing. I was shadowing one of the models and had a small part in the show myself.'

'I can see why,' said Gianni smoothly. 'And this was where you met Luca Di Lazaro for the first time?'

Eve squeezed her eyes shut for a second, summoning every ounce of self-control she possessed to prevent her gaze straying to Raphael. *It was where I met Raphael di Lazaro for the first time,* she wanted to shout. Slumped beside Gianni, he was unsmiling, but more brutally handsome than ever.

'Yes.'

'Thank you, *signorina.*' Gianni spoke with quiet dignity, then allowed a small pause before continuing in a more upbeat tone. 'You say you were commissioned to write this article for—' He paused, looking down at his notes. '*Glitterati* magazine. You are a journalist, then?'

'Not exactly. A friend put my name forward for the job.'

Gianni Orseolo's perfectly arched eyebrows shot up dramatically. 'I see. And what is your real job, Signorina Middlemiss?'

'I'm a research assistant for a professor in Renaissance Poetry at a British university.'

Her heart plummeted to the pit of her stomach as she saw Raphael put his head in his hands in an attitude of utter disbelief.

'Some might say,' Gianni continued thoughtfully, 'that you were somewhat overqualified—academically—for writing a piece of lightweight fashion journalism. Why did your friend put your name forward?'

'Because she knew I had a particular interest in Lazaro.'

'What was that interest, Signorina Middlemiss?'

The musty air of the courtroom was heavy with a sense of expectation. Glancing nervously across at Luca, Eve suddenly realised what was different about his face. It was his nose. A large bump, evidence of a recent break, distorted its once perfect line.

Eve took a deep breath before answering, aware that this was the moment she had been waiting for all these years, but feeling curiously empty now it was here.

'My sister had been spotted by a modelling scout when she was travelling in Florence...' she began hesitantly. 'Someone from Lazaro picked up on this and showed a lot of interest in using her for their shows. She was always quite sure it was just about to happen, but as far as I know nothing came of the modelling thing. But she certainly became quite involved with the people, and went to a lot of the Lazaro parties.'

'When was this?'

'Three and a half years ago.'

Gianni turned away suddenly, and again a tense silence fell upon the waiting court.

Eve couldn't help herself. Inexorably, irresistibly, her gaze found Raphael and her heart gave an almighty lurch.

It was hopeless trying to hate him, or even trying to forget him. She loved him. And it was a life sentence.

Gianni prowled forward to the witness box and handed her a photograph. His eyes bored into hers, willing her to be strong, and unseen by the jury he gave her a swift smile of encouragement. Behind him, Raphael's gaunt face was a mask of icy self-control.

'Signorina Middlemiss, if I may ask you to look at this photograph. I'm afraid its subject matter is a little…intimate, and for that I apologise most sincerely.'

Eve looked down and felt her world tilt slightly. Gripping the brass rail of the witness box she steadied herself, taking a deep gasp of air.

'Eve. You're doing well.' Gianni spoke quietly, so only she could hear, and she looked at him in mute distress. 'Take a moment or two to collect yourself.'

'I'm OK,' she muttered through frozen lips.

'Could you tell the court who the person in the photograph is.'

Eve closed her eyes for a fraction of a second, and struggled to keep her voice steady.

'It's Ellie,' she whispered.

Gianni's eyes beamed encouragement into hers. 'I'm sorry, *signorina*, could you speak up? Who did you say it was?'

With her head held high and tears streaming down her face Eve spoke clearly.

'Ellie.'

There was a sudden noise as Raphael stumbled to his feet. All eyes focused on him as he and Gianni had a swift whispered consultation, after which Gianni faced the bench again and cleared his throat gravely.

'My client informs me that the defendant, Luca Di Lazaro, claims the lady in the photograph is, in fact, you, Signorina Middlemiss, and that you and he enjoyed—how can I put this delicately?—a sexual liaison at his flat before your return to England.'

'No!'

Eve leapt to her feet, the word ringing out through the courtroom, but she was oblivious to the curiosity on the faces of everyone around her. She was aware only of Raphael, and the taut, invisible wires of tension that stretched between them.

'She bears a striking resemblance to you, *signorina*,' said Gianni thoughtfully.

Eve didn't take her eyes off Raphael. A muscle was flickering in his cheek, and his eyes were dark pools of despair.

'She was my twin.'

'Was?' prompted Gianni smoothly. Perfectly controlled, he was like some demonic conductor bringing his orchestra to its rousing climax.

'She died of a heroin overdose. In Florence. Three years ago.'

There was an almost audible sigh as all eyes turned on Luca, but Gianni hadn't finished hammering home his point.

'Hence your interest in Lazaro, Signorina Middlemiss, and your visit to Italy last August. You intended to find the man who had killed your sister.'

But it was as if she hadn't heard him. Staring straight at Raphael, she said, 'I would never have slept with him. I was in love with someone else.'

'I see,' said Gianni.

Beside him, Raphael furiously scribbled something on a sheet of paper on the table in front of them.

Gianni glanced down. 'In that case, *signorina*, may I ask why you left Venice?'

'I found out he didn't love me.'

Gianni's eyes flickered back to Raphael, who was bent over the paper again.

'Er…and what made you think that?'

Eve looked down at her hands, still gripping the railing. Her knuckles were pearl-white beneath the skin.

'He told me he had a business meeting. But I saw him in a café with another woman. He was holding her hands.'

Raphael tried to rise to his feet, but Gianni very firmly pushed him down into his seat and calmly turned back to Eve.

'The lady in question was Catalina Di Souza. Signorina Di Souza has already testified, under oath, that the meeting you witnessed was indeed on a matter of business. She was the person with whom your twin sister shared a flat, and the meeting was to discuss the possibility of bringing Luca di Lazaro to trial for—amongst other things, her death. Signorina Di Souza is still very much affected by it, and the apparent intimacy you witnessed was simply an act of comfort and support.'

Eve had gone very pale. 'I see,' she whispered, through bloodless lips.

Slumped in his chair, Raphael thrust another sheet of paper in front of Gianni, who hesitated for a moment, as if weighing up how to proceed. As he paced thoughtfully towards the witness box Raphael seemed to hold his breath.

'I see that you are expecting a child, signorina. When is it due?'

'*Obiezione!*' Luca's solicitor leapt to his feet. 'This has nothing to do with my client!'

Raphael's eyes burned into her like lasers. Above the commotion from the other bench she spoke directly to him.

'April.'

The elderly judge roused himself with a sigh. 'Objection upheld. Keep your questions to the point, Signor Orseolo, *per favore.*'

Gianni gave him a swift nod, then, seeing the agony on Raphael's face, turned back to Eve. His tone was extremely gentle. 'Who is the father?'

'*Obiezione*! I must protest…!'

'Signor Orseolo! You have been warned to keep your questions relevant to the purpose of the court. This is utterly irrelevant…'

'No, it's not!' Raphael's voice was like the crack of a whip. 'You are.'

A ripple of excitement ran through the court as people craned to catch a glimpse of Raphael's face. Dramatic to the last, Gianni turned his back on the furiously protesting defence team and faced the judge.

'May I ask for a short adjournment? I will continue questioning the witness afterwards.'

The judge eyed him over his small glasses. 'Your witness is

distressed. *Si,* we will adjourn for an hour. But please, Signor Orseolo, rethink your line of questioning.'

The room erupted into noise and chaos as people rose to their feet and filed out. Eve was led from the witness box and taken out into the corridor.

In an instant her kindly police escort was at her side, but Raphael was even quicker. She'd forgotten how tall he was, and how the aura of power and self-control he gave off was both incredibly reassuring and at the same time deeply unsettling. He moved between her and the policeman, his fury thinly disguised behind a veil of courtesy.

'*Scusi, signore.* We have things to discuss.'

Eve lowered her eyes and gave the policeman a small nod. 'Please. We just need a few minutes.'

Raphael leaned back against the wall in a posture that was hauntingly similar to the one in which he'd been standing when she'd first set eyes on him. His eyes had a dangerous, ferocious glitter, and his mouth curled into a sarcastic grimace.

'A few minutes? Is that all it will take, Eve?'

She looked down at her hands. Without thinking she had folded them protectively over her bump. Raphael followed her gaze.

'So. When were you going to tell me?'

Her throat seemed to have constricted so that it was hard to breathe. Or speak.

'I wasn't.'

He let out a sharp hiss and thrust a hand through his hair in that heartbreakingly familiar gesture of exasperation. 'I see. You didn't think that the fact that I am going to be a father was something I might be interested in knowing?'

'By the time I found out I thought you would be happily settled with the girl I saw you kissing! So, no, Raphael, I didn't think it was a piece of news you would greet with unbridled joy.'

'How could you trust me so little?' he spat, springing forward and gripping both her arms in steely fingers. Then he let out a short, bitter laugh. 'Oh, God, how ironic. I spent all the time we were together refusing to allow myself to trust you because I thought you were some sleazy tabloid journalist…' He let go of her arms abruptly and looked away. 'What a bloody mess.'

Eve's hands moved over her stomach, instinctively stroking it. Quietly, imploringly, she said, 'Not completely.' It sounded more like a question than a statement.

For a long moment their gazes held, before Raphael turned away, disgust and despair flooding his face.

'So what are you going to do?' His voice was hollow.

She gave a small shrug, as if the pain caused by his words didn't matter and the small issue of raising a child entirely alone was of no consequence to her whatsoever.

'Manage. Survive.'

He drew in breath sharply and raised clenched fists to his temples. '*Dio,* Eve! What kind of a life is that to bring a child into? *Survive?* How? As a single parent? Going out to work and abandoning the baby—my baby—in some awful daycare?'

She took a step backwards and eyed him coldly. 'Why not? Plenty of people do it.'

'Not with a child of mine.'

Anger surged through her, as hot and energising as a shot of brandy. 'Oh, no. I forgot. Di Lazaros abandon *their* children in very exclusive daycares called public schools. Is that what you're suggesting, Raphael?'

His head jerked back as if she'd slapped him, but he recovered his composure quickly and spoke with icy calm. 'No.' He took a deep breath, looking at her measuringly through narrowed eyes. 'No. The last thing I want is for this child to have the same miserable, screwed-up childhood that I had.' He paused. 'That's why I'm suggesting you come and live here.'

Eve opened her mouth, but suddenly her tongue was dry and there were no words there. Hope flickered somewhere in the darkness where her heart had used to be, but she kept her tone deliberately neutral.

'With you?'

Raphael gave a dry laugh. 'Of course not—as the idea is clearly so abhorrent to you. I'll buy you a flat in a decent area with good schools. But I think it would be best if we got married, to protect the child from…any awkwardness.'

The brave little flame of hope guttered and died, leaving her feeling more alone than ever. 'You're asking me to marry you?' she said dully.

'If you want to put it like that, yes.'

She'd imagined this moment so often in the last six months that at the very least she had expected a full chamber orchestra and someone jumping in front of them with a card saying 'The End' as Raphael bent his head and kissed the living daylights out of her. Not a single one of those fantasies had included the words she now found herself saying.

'No, Raphael.'

She took a couple of steps backwards without taking her eyes from his face. In the half-light it was like an ivory mask—pale, perfect, and completely emotionless.

She turned away and began to walk down the corridor, slowly at first, then with increasing urgency, as if she couldn't wait to get away from him.

Her footsteps echoed off the chilly stone walls, and Raphael tried to avert his gaze, knowing that if he watched her go he would be lost. It was the same feeling he'd had when, as a seven-year-old boy at his mother's funeral, he had not allowed himself to look at the flower-strewn coffin because if he had he'd known he would cry.

And he hadn't. Either then or since.

She had almost reached the end of the corridor when his will-power gave way. Clenching his jaw and thrusting his hands deep into his pockets he looked at her. The cavernous hallway was murky, but her hair shone like distilled sunshine in the winter gloom.

With one hand on the door she paused and looked back at him.
'Sorry,' she said.

The word was like a nail through his heart.

Head down against the rain, and wrapped up in her own despair, Eve almost walked straight past the ancient church, slotted as it was between two much bigger, much grander buildings. Actually, from the outside there wasn't much to see: just a wide arched doorway with a circular stained-glass window in the wall above it. But inside it was beautiful, and dry, and completely deserted.

Numb with cold and misery, she walked slowly down the narrow nave, breathing in the scent of incense and lilies and age. At the altar, rows of votive candles burned in silent tribute to the hopes and prayers of those who had lit them. Hesitantly Eve picked up a taper and held it to the nearest flame, watching it flower into vibrant life for a second before lighting a new candle with it.

'For you, Ellie,' she whispered, holding up the brightly burning taper for a moment before blowing it out with one tender breath. Then she cupped her hands around the little votive, watching her flesh blossom into rosy gold by the light of its tiny flame. 'For you, little baby.'

Resting both hands on her swollen belly, she looked up, then pressed a hand to her mouth as a small, involuntary cry escaped her.

It was almost a relief to feel the tears start to flow. But as she sank down to her knees against a pillar beside the altar rail she wondered if they would ever stop.

She couldn't have said how long she sat like that, but the storm of weeping had blown itself out, and she was just working up the courage to face the rest of her life when a thunderous bang reverberated through the building as the heavy wooden door was forced violently open.

Eve stumbled to her feet. With her heart pounding sickeningly in her chest she peered round the pillar in time to see two men in dark clothes, their faces hidden beneath balaclavas, fling themselves into the church, each brandishing a gun.

Instinct took over. Flattening herself against a pillar, she kept her breathing steady and closed her eyes, feeling the baby lurch inside her as adrenalin pulsed through her veins. She leaned her head back against the cool stone and waited, wondering how much use two masked gunmen would be in an emergency labour situation.

Hysterical laughter built up inside her, but it turned swiftly to terror as she heard the sound of footsteps coming towards her down the nave. She squeezed her eyes more tightly shut, waiting, concentrating every ounce of energy on not making a sound.

The footsteps came closer. Then stopped.

'It's OK! She's here!'

Raphael's voice.

With a whimper of relief Eve opened her eyes to find him standing a few feet away from her. His face was absolutely ashen, his lips white, and he stepped forward and pulled her savagely into his arms, folding her into the safety of his body, cradling her head, then cupping her face in his hands and tilting it upwards towards him. His eyes moved feverishly over her face, as if he wanted to reassure himself she was really there.

'Thank God you're safe.'

'What's happened? Why—?'

He gave a low groan of anguish and pulled her against him again. 'Because you're a witness in a major drugs trial and you're supposed to be under police protection. You've been missing for over two hours. The judge has had to temporarily suspend the trial. We thought you'd been—' He stopped and took in a sharp breath.

Eve's hand flew to her mouth in horror. 'No! I'm so sorry!'

He shook his head. 'It was my fault. I should never have let you go.' He bent his head and pressed his lips to her bright hair, murmuring, 'I thought I'd lost you again before I'd even got the chance to tell you that I love you.'

Eve pulled away and lifted her head to look at him.

'What did you say?'

He stood back, holding her at arm's length. His aristocratic face, with its hard, high cheekbones and beautiful mouth, hadn't quite lost the shadows of anguish and tension, but his dark, narrowed eyes burned with love.

'I love you. I raced off after you walked out like that because I needed to do something to make up for my complete and utter crassness. I went home to get this…' He let go of her for a moment while he pulled something from his pocket. 'And now I want to do it properly, before anything else happens to come between us.'

He held out his hand. In the centre of his palm lay a single solitaire diamond in the shape of a tear.

'Eve—' He pulled her gently back into his arms and kissed her cheekbone, her temple, the corner of her mouth. 'I love you—'

She closed her eyes in bliss and felt the tears spilling out from beneath her lashes. Protesting against the sudden constriction of their bodies pressed together, the baby squirmed inside her.

Raphael gasped. She opened her eyes and saw through a haze of tears the fierce tenderness on his face.

His hands went to her bump—slowly, lovingly moving across it as his eyes stayed fixed on hers.

'I love you both,' he amended softly, smiling that rueful half-smile that seemed to go in at her eyes and move straight down to her pelvis. Taking her hand, speaking in a low voice that only she could hear, he gazed solemnly into her eyes.

'I, Raphael Antonio di Lazaro, take thee, Eve Maria Middlemiss, to be my sweet and incredibly beautiful wedded wife. I will love you, cherish you—' He broke off, raising her hand to his lips and placing a kiss on the tip of her index finger. 'Comfort you, protect you…' He kissed her middle finger. 'Honour you and make endless fantastic love with you for all the days of my life.' Holding up her third finger, he slid the ring onto it. 'If you'll have me?'

Through a shimmering veil of tears Eve looked around her at the altar, and the effigy of Christ above it, and gave a soft laugh. 'I think it's too late. I think you've done it and there's no going back. I now pronounce us husband and wife.'

'Good,' said Raphael firmly. 'But let's do it again formally anyway. In the meantime, may I kiss the—'

He didn't finish the question. But the answer was undoubtedly yes.

EPILOGUE

RAPHAEL tiptoed to the top of the stairs and paused, a slow smile spreading across his face. From through the slightly open door at the end of the hallway he could hear Eve singing very softly.

Madame Butterfly.

Downstairs, the low murmur of conversation was punctuated by the occasional burst of laughter and the clink of champagne glasses. Their 'formal' wedding, as Eve laughingly called it, was in full swing, with Antonio—on sparkling form—holding court at its centre. Raphael felt sure that he wouldn't be missed for a while.

He pushed open the nursery door. Eve, humming languidly now, looked up at him and smiled.

He felt his stomach tighten. With desire, and also with that primitive protective instinct that she teased him about, but which he knew he could never quite extinguish.

She was curled into the armchair next to the cot, one arm cradling the dark head of Eleanor Isabella di Lazaro against her bared breast.

Little Ellie-Bella, as her doting godmother Lou had nick-named her, had inherited her grandmother's delicate, dark-haired beauty and her aunt's sense of naughtiness and fun. Now, after an afternoon spent playing to the wedding crowd, she was un-usually placid.

'Is she asleep already?' he murmured.

'Mmm...' Eve moved the baby slightly, so that her small mouth relinquished the nipple with a tiny, contented sigh. Her dark lashes swept down over her rosy, milk-damp cheeks, and for a moment both her parents gazed down at her with rapt adoration.

'I think that's got to be a record,' Eve whispered, smiling. 'I hadn't even got to the end of the aria.'

'Perfect. No one will be expecting us downstairs for a long, long time.'

With infinite tenderness Raphael took the baby from her mother's arms and pressed a kiss on the soft dark hair before laying her into her cot. Then he turned to Eve with a smile that made her heart turn over.

He held out a hand and pulled her gently to her feet, allowing himself a moment to marvel all over again at her beauty in the simple sheath of heavy cream silk. Her clear turquoise-green eyes sparkled wickedly as he brought his lips down to hers.

'You know, Raphael, I'm not sure,' she whispered against his mouth, so that he could hear but not see her smile. 'Married sex might not be as exciting as it was before. Maybe we should just go downstairs?'

'Actually, Signora di Lazaro,' he said softly, sweeping her up into his arms in a rustle of silk, muffling her cries of pleasure and laughter with his lips as he carried her to the door. 'I'm afraid you're wrong. Married sex is *even better*. And if you don't believe me I'll just have to prove it to you.'

And he did.

Twice.

Men who can't be tamed...or so they think!

If you love strong, commanding men,
you'll love this brand-new miniseries.

Meet the guy who breaks the rules to get exactly
what he wants, because he is...

HARD-EDGED & HANDSOME

He's the man who's impossible to resist....

RICH & RAKISH

He's got everything—and needs nobody...
until he meets one woman....

He's RUTHLESS!

In his pursuit of passion; in his world the winner takes all!

Coming in November:

THE BILLIONAIRE'S CAPTIVE BRIDE

by Emma Darcy
Book #2676

Coming in December:

BEDDED, OR WEDDED?

by Julia James
Book #2684

Brought to you by your favorite Harlequin Presents authors!

HP12679

REQUEST YOUR FREE BOOKS!

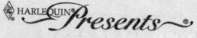 HARLEQUIN *Presents*®

 PASSION GUARANTEED SEDUCTION

2 FREE NOVELS PLUS 2 FREE GIFTS!

YES! Please send me 2 FREE Harlequin Presents® novels and my 2 FREE gifts. After receiving them, if I don't wish to receive any more books, I can return the shipping statement marked "cancel." If I don't cancel, I will receive 6 brand-new novels every month and be billed just $3.80 per book in the U.S., or $4.47 per book in Canada, plus 25¢ shipping and handling per book and applicable taxes, if any*. That's a savings of close to 15% off the cover price! I understand that accepting the 2 free books and gifts places me under no obligation to buy anything. I can always return a shipment and cancel at any time. Even if I never buy another book from Harlequin, the two free books and gifts are mine to keep forever.

106 HDN EEXK   306 HDN EEXV

Name _____ (PLEASE PRINT) _____

Address _____ Apt. # _____

City _____ State/Prov. _____ Zip/Postal Code _____

Signature (if under 18, a parent or guardian must sign) _____

Mail to the Harlequin Reader Service®:

IN U.S.A.: P.O. Box 1867, Buffalo, NY 14240-1867
IN CANADA: P.O. Box 609, Fort Erie, Ontario L2A 5X3

Not valid to current Harlequin Presents subscribers.

Want to try two free books from another line?
Call 1-800-873-8635 or visit www.morefreebooks.com.

* Terms and prices subject to change without notice. NY residents add applicable sales tax. Canadian residents will be charged applicable provincial taxes and GST. This offer is limited to one order per household. All orders subject to approval. Credit or debit balances in a customer's account(s) may be offset by any other outstanding balance owed by or to the customer. Please allow 4 to 6 weeks for delivery.

Your Privacy: Harlequin is committed to protecting your privacy. Our Privacy Policy is available online at www.eHarlequin.com or upon request from the Reader Service. From time to time we make our lists of customers available to reputable firms who may have a product or service of interest to you. If you would prefer we not share your name and address, please check here. ☐

HP07